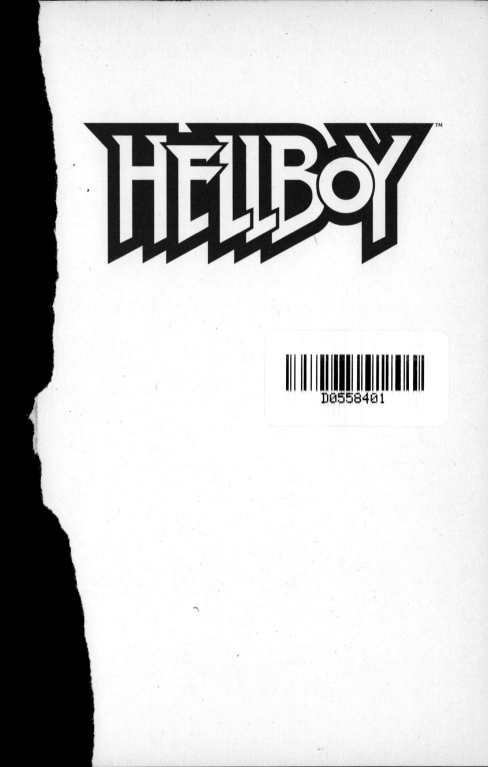

D0558401

EMERALD HELL

TOM PICCIRILLI

Hellboy created by Mike Mignola

Dark Horse Books®
Milwaukie

Book design by Krystal Hennes
Cover design by Lia Ribacchi
Cover illustration by Mike Mignola
Front cover color by Dave Stewart

Published by Dark Horse Books
A division of Dark Horse Comics
10956 SE Main Street
Milwaukie, OR 97222

darkhorse.com

Library of Congress Cataloging-in-Publication Data

Piccirilli, Tom.
  Hellboy: Emerald hell / Tom Piccirilli ; created by Mike Mignola. -- 1st Dark Horse Books ed.
    p. cm.
  ISBN-13: 978-1-59582-141-6
  1. Hellboy (Fictitious character : Mignola)--Fiction. I. Mignola, Michael. II. Title. III. Title:
Emerald hell.
  PS3566.I266H46 2008
  813'.54--dc22
                                        2007049449

First Dark Horse Books Edition: February 2008
ISBN 978-1-59582-141-6

Printed in the United States of America

10 9 8 7 6 5 4 3 2 1

For Gerard Houarner, who introduced me to Big Red

Special thanks need to go out to:
Christopher Golden,
for his editorial skills and general midwifery of the novel.

Victoria Blake,
for overall assistance right down the line.

Guillermo del Toro,
for bringing HB to the big screen and giving us fans what
we've wanted for years.

And, of course, Mike Mignola,
for letting me run riot in his groovy world once again.

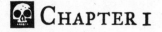 CHAPTER I

Hellboy came to the crossroads.

He'd been sitting in the back of the pickup for nearly a hundred and sixty miles while the others passed a jug of moonshine around and told their stories. The pickup couldn't do better than forty on the rutted dirt and gravel roads so it took most of the afternoon before they finally passed into Georgia.

Their folksy tales started off light and humorous and full of character, but eventually came around to death and ghosts, as he knew they would. Hellboy said very little but listened intently, especially when they got to talking about Bliss Nail and his six silent daughters. It had the ring of truth to it and he asked a few questions. The answers made him nod. He told them to take him as close by the Nail home as they could get him.

They said they'd drop him at the edge of Enigma, a swamp town that had been ebbing since before Sherman put the flame to Atlanta, but just wouldn't die. They were out of work and looking to hook up with some moon runners down that way anyhow.

The world turned even greener around him when a powerful summer shower came rushing out of the east. The others managed to crowd together into the cab and he sat alone staring into the marshy prairies of emerald cypress. Heavy winds stirred the catclaw briars and underbrush, thick branches parting as if a hidden audience was coming forward to take a peek. The storm rocked the pickup for a few miles but ended quickly.

The truck pulled over and the others piled into the back again. One had a banjo and another a washboard and they began to softly play and sing. Sunlight skimmed off the tupelo trees, casting a fiery green glow against the woven layers of deeper bog shadow. Hellboy dozed for a while listening to their music and thought he heard a baby crying.

A half hour later, they told him they'd reached Enigma and he unloaded. The toothless old man who owned the truck spit out some chaw and asked, "You want a last tap'a lightnin'?"

"No thanks," Hellboy said.

"Son, it don't take but two seconds to see you got yourself a sorrowful accounting. You watch your passage 'round these here swamps. They got a habit of finding their way into your heart. There's bad will in them waters." He pointed south, and Hellboy noticed the old man's fingertips had been chewed away from sixty years of having his hands in the mash barrels. "That direction, no more'n four five mile, and you'll find yourself in the Nail fold. Don't be lettin' any'a their black luck rub off on you none."

Hellboy thanked them all and started south while they turned west and disappeared up a dusty track into the lengthening shadows. When he got to the center of the crossroads he stood poised for a moment waiting to see if anything would come out and make a play for him. According to legend, this was where you came to meet the devil. He checked the brush land and thickening jungle around him, toed the mud, and scanned the sky.

"Anybody got a problem?" he called as the sunset bled out in the distance. "Anyone got anything to say to me?"

When nothing showed up, he continued along the trail.

As darkness set in, the mist drifted off the deep acreage of sugarcane that flattened back to the surrounding slough and mire. Blooming loblolly bushes, palmettos, and thick fields sprouting a type of

Still not even twenty, her long brown hair was edged with strands of silver. It sort of matched Lament's white streak. These two kids with such youthful vigor and intensity, but somehow brushed by age, tragedy, and worldliness.

She and Lament held each other and moved in close, cheek to cheek, his mouth at her ear whispering, her lips pressing along his jaw line. Lament eased his hand over her bulging belly, and Hellboy knew what would be coming next.

He started to count off . . . one, two, three, four . . . and then looked over at Ma'am McCulver and saw that she was doing the same thing. They both let out a sigh just as a growl of thunder grumbled overhead.

"I couldn't wait for you," Sarah said to Lament. "I felt the devil's breath on my neck and knew we had to get on out of Enigma. I knew you must be worryin' somethin' dreadful but I thought it best to move on."

"I know that," he told her. "I'm sorry I was late gettin' to you. We had some trials along the way. I wouldn't have gotten through at all if not for this fella right here though."

Lament put his hand on Hellboy's shoulder and drew him closer. Sarah smiled at him and said, "Thank you for what you did for my John."

It was the kind of thing that made you go, Aw shucks, 'twern't nuthin', but Hellboy resisted. It was harder than he expected. "I was just doing what I had to do. Someone has to."

"Ain't no man's mere service to save another. It's a calling of the courageous."

He didn't know what to say to that so he let it go by. "You and your friends are the brave ones, battling through the swamp in your, ah, condition."

"We had us a time, with Becky Sue all but ready to have her baby girl in the bottom of the skiff, but thank the Lord, she managed to hold off." She turned to Lament. "The dreams, John."

flower he'd never seen before filled the evening air with an assertive but sweet fragrance.

The Nail family lived in an antediluvian mansion that had been built long before the separation of states. He saw where it had been rebuilt after Civil War strife and he could feel the dense and bloody history in the depths of the house. He glanced up at a row of large windows on the second floor and saw six lovely pale women staring down at him.

An elderly servant with a balding head and thick white pork-chop sideburns answered the door before Hellboy could even knock. That's the way the dead did it, trying to get one step ahead of you. Showing you they were always at the ready, waiting be-hind glass panes and cracked slats, aware but unwilling to come out when challenged.

The houseman asked him his business at the Nail home and Hellboy said, "I'm not the damn plumber, Jeeves."

It made the old guy draw his chin back and pull a face. His tidy uniform hung off his thin frail frame, the black suit-coat shabby but well brushed, his frayed shirt collar clean and starched. Maybe times weren't so good for the Nail clan either.

The houseman gestured for him to follow and led him down lengthy corridors past Colonial furniture and glass cases containing medals, swords, and antique guns. No photos anywhere. Nothing very modern that he could see. He started getting the feeling he'd been suckered by the spirits again and just imagined the houseman was really a skeleton and the girls upstairs were long murdered.

The home seeped age and sovereignty. The walls were filled with oil paintings going back a century and a half of wars, showing angry-faced little men wearing flashy uniforms and carrying sabers, their lips curled into the smallest of bitter smiles.

The portraits whispered to Hellboy. Chanting in melodic yet hissing voices, really trying to get under his skin. They mentioned a few of his major failures, the towns he'd wrecked, the people

"I suppose not. Why you wanna help the likes'a me and mine?"

"It's my job."

"Who in the ass end'a creation got a job like that?"

Sometimes you just couldn't win, Hellboy thought. You could reach out and pull a drowning guy from the rioting ocean and he'd still give you crap for not bringing a towel.

Hellboy shrugged. "I do. You got a problem with that?"

It was the right thing to say, and it broke the mood. Bliss Nail let loose with a booming laugh that, despite himself, Hellboy enjoyed hearing. The comment was sincere.

"You like catfish, son?"

"I don't know," Hellboy told him. "I've never had any."

"What kind'a place you come from that don't ever serve catfish?"

"Connecticut."

Bliss Nail considered this. "That don't hardly sound civilized."

"I suppose it depends."

"On what?"

"On whether you're from Connecticut."

Not exactly true. He had no real home. He'd been born in England and had traveled most of his life, first with the Army and later with the Bureau for Paranormal Research and Defense. Headquarters was in Connecticut. When he thought of home, that's where he thought of it being, as much as it could be for him.

Bliss Nail called in Waldridge, who placed heaping portions of food on Hellboy's plate, aiming the catfish eyes first toward him.

"Them shards of horn on yer head?" Bliss Nail asked after the houseman had retreated.

"Yeah."

"You got 'em mounted someplace?"

"No."

"Well why not, son? They'd fetch a pretty dollar on the market."

Hellboy didn't want to think about what kind of market there might be for horns, or for his mounted animal head, so he said,

"How about if we just let that go for now?"

Nodding, Bliss Nail took another sip of wine. His gaze grew distant as he tried to put his troubles in some proper order. Hellboy knew this was the toughest part, just getting them to find the beginning of their own tales. He himself wouldn't have an easy time of it either.

"You know who I am?" Bliss Nail asked.

"Bliss Nail. I thought we had established that already."

"The name mean anything to you?"

Hellboy stared down at the plates of food in front of him. The fish stared back at him. It had dangling tendrils like whiskers. They were right, this thing really did look like a cat. He wondered about people who could eat this fish and not think about Fluffy meowing and purring in the corner. He thought he'd rather have pancakes. "Not much."

"I'm the first to admit I'm a touch vain, so that hurts me some. What do you know?"

Hellboy held back a sigh and said, "Why don't you just tell me your story?"

Bliss Nail's features folded in on themselves and he seemed ready to cut loose, but at the last moment he reined himself in and let out a brief, cold laugh. "I reckon I will. I have seven girls. Six of them upstairs, ranging in age from thirty to forty, their mama almost three decades underground. Those six ain't spoken a word in near twenty years. Not a whisper, no matter how many specialists, psychiatrists, or ministers looked in on 'em. And there's been more than a few, that's the sweet truth. But tonight—"

Drifting again, Bliss Nail tried to sip more wine but the goblet was empty. He didn't refill it and didn't set it down. He turned to the dark windows, staring outside so intently that Hellboy thought the guy might throw himself through the glass.

So Hellboy cut to the chase and said, "Tonight something changed, right?" His presence alone was generally enough to stir things up. "Tonight you heard them speak."

"That's right," Bliss Nail said. "As soon as the sun set they all come down and ringed 'round the dining table and spoke three names. All together, like they was a choir singin' a hymn. It was powerful eerie and heartliftin' and lovely too, because I been missin' their voices. Their song, sung with their souls. Just those three names. Yours. My enemy's. And that of a young man I don't hardly know, but who's got a reckoning with my family."

"Go on."

"My exquisite girls are cursed. Or better said, I am cursed, and my daughters due to me. Not only don't they speak, but they can't carry children."

Hellboy thought, There it is, the reason I heard the baby crying.

"They're breathtaking women, with kind and gracious hearts. They don't talk but they have a great deal to say. They write letters that put the Psalms to shame. Before the story got about in town, the oldest three had intendeds who doted hand and heel and loved them dearly. But all the men have left now. They've run out because my daughters can't carry on a family name in a family way. It's me that poisons them. They don't deserve this burden. A man wants to put a knife to me, I'll meet him head-on. But to do this to unborn—to never born—children, that's an unholy blight."

"But your seventh daughter?"

"Sarah."

The only one he'd given a name to. "She's had a child?"

"Me and her mama, we wasn't married. My wife was long gone by then. Sarah's mama, she was a fine woman, but—"

Sliding out of his chair, Bliss Nail moved to a liquor cart behind him and poured himself a brandy. He slugged the first tumbler's worth back, then filled it again. He remembered his manners then and gestured at Hellboy, who waved it off.

Reseating himself, Bliss Nail said, "But she was married during our time together. Her husband, he spent long periods on the road. Months and years away from her without a word. When he came home and found her with child, he murdered her with a hatchet."

"Christ."

"Since Sarah didn't take my name, she avoided the plague on me and mine. She was raised by another couple in town, but last year they died too. Natural-like. Because Sarah was raised up out of my shadow, she grew strong and happy and a chatterbox. I deceived the ill will aimed toward me and mine. She's nineteen and pregnant now and about to bear my only grandchild."

Every man had to tell his own story in his own way, but Hellboy knew Bliss Nail was editing himself, leaving out his own sins. Hellboy thought he could brace him a little, see what he could squeeze loose, but figured in the end it would just hurt the investigation. "Does Sarah know you're her real father?"

"I don't know. We've never spoken to one another. I feared if we did the blight would set upon her."

"Who cursed you and yours? Who bewitched you twenty years ago?"

"A dead man."

Should've seen that one coming, Hellboy thought. "And who might he be?"

"The husband. The man who killed Sarah's mama. He was a preacher, a travelin' minister, famous in these parts and all across the swamps and the deep South. He once had the power of the Word, and anyone who heard him speak could feel it. Some called him a healer though I don't know if he ever made such a claim. But he performed wonders and knew great secrets. They said they saw him with angels. A blessed gospel singer and a staunch man of God."

"Until you fooled around with his wife."

It made Bliss Nail raise his chin, straighten in his seat, and let loose with an agonized warble as if he'd just been punched in the kidneys. He reared like he was going to leave his chair, maybe take a poke at Hellboy. His face went through three shades of purple and finally settled on grape.

Hellboy waited. He heard the girls roaming up the corridor, all rustling of silk and lace. Finally Bliss Nail let out a groan and sank in on himself, visibly deflating. "Like I said, my sins ought to be my hardship alone. He once had another name but the one they all spoke together, though I'd never heard it before, was Brother Jester. Still I knew it was him."

Brother Jester. The name was repeated six times out in the hall-way, where the silent bewitched daughters were forced to speak. They wafted past the open doorway like wraiths, too lovely, too thin, and too pale. For a moment he wondered what their letters might be like to read, and imagined bundles of scented pages tied with bows, never mailed and never opened. He fought to contain himself, but his great stone-like hand clenched into a fist at his side. His journey had made him a little maudlin and edgy. He wanted to beat the crap out of something.

"He been gone from Enigma for years," Bliss Nail said. "There was rumors, for a time, that he'd gone insane and was now using his voice to kill. He knew secrets that set brother against brother, that made husbands rise up against their wives and children. But then the rumors stopped and I thought we'd never hear from him again. I reckoned he was dead. But if Brother Jester is back in Enigma, I fear for Sarah's safety. He'll extend his curse or cut her down like a field of ripe cane."

Waldridge entered and began to clear the plates. When he got to the untouched catfish in front of Hellboy he made a face. Hellboy didn't mind, he was just glad to have the damn thing stop looking at him.

"There's war in my family's veins," Bliss Nail said. "We all been soldiers right down the line. If I thought it would help, I'd take a Bowie and a Colt .45 and go after him myself. But—"

"But you're smart enough to know that you're the one who somehow gave him his power," Hellboy finished. "You made him what he is."

Bliss Nail's hard features had softened considerably during their talk, and the fierceness had gone out of the man. His steel-gray eyes were no longer steeped with strength, but accommodated only loss and fear. It happened like that when you caught a full jolt of memories that showed you exactly what you were and what you'd once done.

"So where is Sarah? I'll go look after her."

"She's with Mrs. Hoopkins. Out at Mrs. Hoopkins's Home for Unwed Wayward Teenage Mothers & Peanut Farm."

Hellboy wanted to say, You people. You people, Christ.

"When is she due?"

"A matter of days."

"What about the third name your daughters spoke?"

"Sarah's beau, my grandchild's father, I believe. He's a back-woods traveler who wanders the Appalachians the same way Jester did and maybe still does. There's bountiful rumors about him too. They say he's got a touch of magic to him. I don't know if that's true or not, but I take note of such talk. I hear tell he's back in town. His name is John Lament. That's what they said. *Lament.*"

At Lament's name the six nameless daughters spoke and drifted past the door once again, as if this was a ballet that they had re-hearsed many times before. Lovely and ethereal, like wisps of white smoke. He found himself wanting to hear their voices through their written words.

"Name your price," Bliss Nail said. "What you want for this aid in my needful hour? You only stumbled upon my ills."

"I did. But that's how these things happen."

"You help and I'm in your debt. You fix the cost and I'll pay it."

"How about the price of a bus ticket to Connecticut?"

Bliss Nail frowned. "That all?"

"I don't much like hitchhiking."

"You have my word."

Hellboy guessed that before this was all over, he'd find out ex-actly how much that was worth.

"Okay, so how do I get to this peanut farm anyway?"

"Waldridge will drive you," Bliss Nail said, and his silent daughters continued staring, waiting for their otherworldly sentence to
be lifted. Their voices to return, the house to be filled with the
sound of children. As Hellboy stood and walked from the room,
they each came to him, lithe and pallid, eyes ashen and lovely faces
stern with pain. They floated past with their silk dresses trailing, and
one of the silent daughters, perhaps the one who'd waved to him
on the stairway before, who looked too similar to her sisters for him
to tell her from the others, pressed a soft hand to his cheek before
gliding away with the rest.

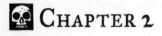# CHAPTER 2

Brother Jester, slave to God's pettiest whims, returned to the town of Enigma, that place of his former life, his eventual undoing, and his own death.

The hunger visited again. He found a crushed possum in the road and began to remove what few guts remained in it. He only ate what the Lord provided and only what he found offered to him in the road. It was both a measure of penance and an act of defiance. Daring Heaven to whittle him down farther, if that was his fate. When there was no food, he ate his rage.

While Brother Jester could starve, he couldn't die.

The moon shone down in a burnished silver rippling. He had no shadow when he walked, but he had many in his mind. As he'd preached his way back and forth across thousands of miles of the American South, occasionally retracing his steps from church to church, through a ghost town or swamp village, he'd send the shadows out among the crowds and they'd return with hidden truths. It was the way of the Lord.

Sometimes he spoke these secrets aloud in his devastated voice, letting a cuckold know which men his wife had slept with. Periodically he held back words that might ease decades of bad blood among families or carry an afflicted soul up from the void. He could only do so much, and took pleasure in doing no more for others than was ever done for him. We all have our blood to let.

He worked his will among the people as God did, treating them no better or worse than Heaven ever had. Some died at ease, others did not. He reveled in their faithlessness as much as he did in their courage. On their deathbeds, he murmured their corruptions and trickery to them and watched the turmoil and terror bloom in their eyes just as the light of life faded from them.

It was, in its own way, quite glorious.

As Jester continued walking, taking his first bite of raw possum, he heard the woman whimpering out in the morass.

He moved off the road and pressed through the palm fronds and scrub oak. He eased into darkness and his shadows awakened. The ground grew muddier and the glowing cypress grew thicker, the hanging moss stretched out above. He heard laughter and hunkered down behind a stand of sprouting sassafras.

Two handsome, golden-haired men stood at the shore of a hillock of slough watching a middle-aged woman slowly sink into the mire. Her arms flailed once and she let out a sob, but could do no more than that. All the fight had already gone out of her, blood in her eyes as she cried out a name that sounded like "Henry."

Two scut-backed bull gators swam through the slime toward her, their powerful tails slashing deep black wakes behind them.

The men crouched and pawed through clothes and the contents of the woman's luggage and purse, letting out whoops of joy when they found fifty dollars in cash.

"I gonna get me a new shirt and go out dancin' Friday night," one said.

"You can't dance worth a lick, but you can use you some new clothes, 'specially some undergarments, whether you two-step in 'em or not."

Brother Jester sent his own darkness among the two killers and the dying woman, watching the shadows flap free as their feathery touch brushed the raised, knotted flesh of his scarred throat. They returned momentarily with knowledge of love and crimes that had been, and would be, completely buried in these swamps. It added to his anguished heart.

The woman's name was Marcie Andrews, a saleswoman on her way down to Jacksonville for a Mary Kay Cosmetics convention. She was a top earner in Raleigh and wanted to win a pink Cadillac for selling more product than anyone else in the region. She had stopped several times during her trip to hold impromptu sales pitches with various waitresses at truck stop diners and five-and-dime cashiers.

Sixteen cases of lipstick, eye shadow, rouge, pancake powder, and other necessities for a woman's morning ritual of beautifying were packed in the back of her Ford. Her husband Henry had told her not to push the Ford past sixty for fear of throwing a rod, but the more she stopped the further behind in her schedule she got, and the faster she drove to make up for lost time.

Already she'd sold another $227.48 worth of cosmetics, which she just knew was going to earn her that Caddy. Then Henry would surely be happy and might even take her on a second honeymoon like he'd been promising for the last twenty-eight years of marriage. The first honeymoon had been three days at the Whispering Pines Motel outside of Rosestock, South Carolina where he'd mostly gone fishing with the motel manager and another newly wedded husband, and Marcie and the other newly wedded wife mostly browsed at the little souvenir shop and read recipe magazines together.

She threw a rod two miles outside Enigma and sat behind the wheel flustered and cussing, wondering where in the hell she was going to find someone to help her in this swamp burg. Her tears cut quarter-inch-deep twin channels down her heavily made-up face and, gesticulating helplessly to the sky, she began to walk the road.

In their Dodge Charger, the Ferris boys found her that way, alone and about a half mile from her truck. They offered to haul the

Ford to the nearest repair station, and Marcie, so taken with their chiseled, winsome features, didn't start to get worried until they were already deep in the river bottoms and bog land.

The boys didn't have to do anything more than toss her out the door into the morass. Marcie's penchant for fried foods and bon-bons hadn't done her figure much good, and after five minutes of trying to dog paddle out in the muck, she was breathless and ready to go under. If she was lucky, she might drown before the gators dragged her off to gator ground and rolled her down in the mud, letting her ripen wedged and broken between logs. It might take days to die that way.

Brother Jester parted the high-standing sassafras and stepped into view. Showing mercy, as the Lord sometimes did, he was filled with prophecy and said to the woman in his ruined voice, "Henry will soon be with you before the eternal divine presence, Marcie. When he hears of your death he'll shoot himself in the head with his father's Army .45. You'll be together come Judgment Day in the light of Christ's peace and beauty."

Marcie tipped to one side, dying but still worried that her hair was getting dirty and the nice French curls that had cost her eigh-teen dollars down at Iris Connifer's House of Beauteous Bouffants were getting bugs in them.

But before the dark waters filled her mouth she whimpered, "Help me . . . oh no Henry . . . no . . . don't . . ."

The bull gator took her by the legs and yanked her under right then. Jester saw it would be hours before she would pass, as the gators jammed her beneath a hill of brambles to rot and tenderize. She wouldn't be eaten until Tuesday.

Jester bowed his head and said a prayer.

The Ferris boys stared at him and saw what the rest of the world saw. A seasoned, weathered, gaunt man with parchment-white skin, wearing a dusty frock coat, string-tie, and flat black hat of the old-time traveling ministers.

"Son, you done messed with us now," Deeter Ferris said. "Better to fling yourself in the mud your own self than cross paths with us."

His brother Duffy pointed to the water. "Go on and get in there. Don't you make me dirty my snakeskin boots none."

"That wouldn't be right at'all."

"Not'all."

"I know who you are," Brother Jester said. "Duffy and Deeter Ferris, who killed your own parents when you were but ten-year- and eleven-year-old bucks. And you haven't stopped your back- woods murdering since. You've masked your evil with your charm and comeliness, so no one dares accuse you."

The Ferris boys didn't act surprised to hear their ugliest and most intimate truth spoken aloud. Enigma was a town of many open secrets.

Deeter stroked the golden stubble on his chin and said, "This preacher sound like he been garglin' hot asphalt."

"Good that he ain't bein' loud, my ears is still ringin' from that woman's yodelin'. Why you sound like that, preacher?"

"I was hanged," Jester said.

The Ferris brothers burst out laughing. Duffy asked, "Well, son, who done hanged you?"

"I don't remember."

"Reckon you might recollect a thing like that."

Deeter moved forward. "Reverend, you made the worst mis- take in your whole dang life, not haulin' ass while you had the chance." He drew a Bowie knife that glinted with shreds of moon- light. "Lord almighty, now ain't you one sad sight, boy. Been a while since you had yourself some biscuits and gravy, ain't it. You won't hardly make a decent dessert for them bulls."

A six-inch skinning blade appeared in Duffy's hand. "You is surely one ugly sumbitch, Reverend. We doin' you a favor sendin' you off to Heaven 'fore you ain't nothin' but a walkin' skin-bag'a corruption and bones."

How true, Jester thought. Such luminous gospel cannot be hidden even from ignorant degenerates as this.

They approached easily with their weapons drawn, the violence and butchery in them large and majestic, which Brother Jester found refreshing.

He held up a hand and a faint crackle of black energy played between his fingers, dancing across his debased flesh, before he stretched out his palm and the power moved from him toward the killers.

Here was the capricious will of God. As often distant and oblivious as it was pure and obliging. Here was the strength of ten thousand prayers spoken in hope and belief, and ten thousand more from the heart of his loss and hatred.

"Hellfire, son," Duffy called. "What you got there?"

Jester afforded himself a grin. "Heaven-fire."

He clenched his hand and the cords of mystic power tightened around their bodies while they screamed. It was an ugly passionate sound, perhaps loud enough for Marcie Andrews to hear down where she moaned trapped and broken in the catclaw briars and tussocks of weeds. The black energy wove about the Ferris boys and stung at them like wasps. It tore and delved and slithered through their ears to heat their brains. It dug at their tongues and knew all their words. It skittered against their knives and the blades turned red-hot in the emerald darkness. Both cried out, "*God*—"

We all call for God before our deaths, Jester thought, all except himself, of course. Which is perhaps why he was so blessed and so damned.

His shadows found all their secrets and weaknesses and raked their excruciating places. The brothers, like all righteous penitents, went to their knees, bleeding and sobbing and begging.

"I may have use for you two," Jester said.

Once he had been a man like other men, but perhaps with a greater will to serve Heaven than most. He preached the holy word and sought to save lives that had gone to shambles. The road whispered for him to follow and he traveled the land giving witness and testament. He had a lush, compelling voice and would sing at tent revivals. His words, a gift from on high, brought peace and joy, and then, by turns, prophecy and tongues.

Eventually, through another boon, he began to heal the sick. The crippled, diseased, and maimed came to him in long processions, winding through the marshes and villages and towns, hobbling in along the dirt tracks, the blind following his voice.

He had the love of a good woman at home and he always returned to her, in time. When he returned they would picnic down by the bottoms and make love in the juniper. When the Lord called for him to move on again, she understood.

His last few years as a mortal man had been busy ones. He was away from home more than ever. Building churches, improving schools, inviting doctors to create clinics. Mending those he could and consoling those he could not. The flocks gathered to him. No matter how often they saw the miracle of each new day, and were blessed with life and family, they needed to be reminded of the Word.

There were more ill children to attend and souls to save. So many that when he spotted the orphan boy in the swamp revival during an all-night sing, and heard the child sing and preach with a golden voice even more commanding than his own, he knew he would mentor and cultivate the boy's skills.

After those long months traveling the hills and the swamps, growing to love the boy as a son, he returned to Enigma strong and tan and full of conviction to find his wife holding a newborn baby girl.

He remembered that moment as one of overwhelming elation, so much so that he rushed to her and threw his arms around her. It wasn't until he noticed his wife's terrified expression that he realized he couldn't be the father. He'd been away for more than a year.

Brother Jester could no longer recall his wife's name, or his own at that time, because for so long it made him suffer and groan to even think of them. But he spoke her name then, whatever it had been, and, with the pieces of his heart twisting inside him, he looked at the baby and wanted to kill it.

His wife spoke his name, whatever it was, and said, "You love God more than you do me."

It wasn't a question. It needed no answer. But he felt compelled to say, "Yes." As if there could be any other response from him. As if there should be.

"He's a selfish god, is what He is," she continued, "and I'm a selfish woman. I need a man wants me more than anything else. Who comes home to be a husband."

Jester began crying, smiling sickly, unable to stop. "But we were bound before—"

"You haven't spent more than a week at home in the five years we've been married. How bound does that make you to me?"

He didn't know what to say or what to do. The full sweeping call of his rage had not struck yet. His tears fell and he staggered about the room, occasionally lurching toward the baby as if to take her, and then moving off again. He stumbled into furniture. He hugged the boy and then shoved him aside. There were pictures of Jesus on the wall staring.

Brother Jester asked who the father was.

His wife wouldn't answer.

But even then, as his path to destruction widened before him, with no possibility of avoidance, his power was rising. He went to his knees before his wife, chewing his lips, blood filling his mouth.

Shadows drifted. Angels moved through the air and knew him—*Azrael, Adonai, Ariel, Anafiel*—their wings unfurling and the light brush of black feathers touching his cheek, their shadows crossing his racked body like scourges.

The knowledge became his because it was nothing but a greater torture. And from such pain came purification. His mind filled with white light and the answers to his questions.

Bliss Nail, the rotten rich man who already had six daughters. They were always laughing and gabbing about town, driven about in a huge town car, with a chauffeur who tipped his cap to everyone he passed.

The baby girl merely stared at Jester, smiling toothlessly, and then reached for him and grabbed hold of his finger.

Jester scowled at his wife's child, wanting it dead.

The boy, standing behind him and holding a handful of roses to present to the woman, said with true understanding, "The Lord's work sometimes ain't easy on His servants. We do our best but it ain't always good enough."

In his heartbreak, and in the awakening of his true nature, Jester had almost forgotten about the boy. His protégé, his almost-son.

Brother Jester said, "Quiet, boy, you don't know anything about what this means."

"I reckon I do, and it's you who's done lost your way. I see it in your eyes. They're brimmin' with hate. It's not too late. Ask forgiveness."

"Like hell!"

And then, like the striking of a hammer, Jester's skull nearly burst with his black grief and righteous wrath, his need to die and his need to kill. He screamed and the baby began to cry, and the wife backed out of the room, and the boy dropped the roses.

Jester remembered running for the shed and finding the hatchet there. The shadows of lost archangels lashing him along like a whipped animal.

The boy had tried to stop him. The child's faith was fearsome and forceful, even the angels drew back from the boy, confused and uncertain. But the boy was only eight years old and Jester struck out with the hatchet and left the child crumpled in the dust, his forehead cracked and bleeding.

Returning to his wife, who was on the phone pleading for her lover to aid her, Jester casually twirled the hatchet, the blade dark with a splash of the boy's blood. Bliss Nail's voice came through the line loudly, and in the background there was the sound of girls squabbling and yakking. He grabbed up the phone and said, "Bliss Nail, you'll have a silent home now."

Then he proceeded to murder his wife.

She didn't struggle, her hands raised as if to scratch at his eyes. But she never did claw at him, as if too disgusted to touch him now, even if it might save her life. He left the infant in its cradle, willing it to die but unable to reach out and break its neck or use the hatchet. And how he had tried. He'd stared at his hands for minutes, until they turned black and began to spark. But for some reason, despite his rage, he couldn't place his fists in the cradle and do the deed.

After that, his memory became a haze. He remembered awakening once at the end of a noose, his body swaying, laughing to himself because he wasn't dead. Then he felt small hands on him. His next recollection was three days later. He was bent in the road chewing on the headless body of an egret. There were feathers in his mouth, and a group of children stood across from him, whimpering, too frightened to even run.

His once-strong voice, which had brought peace and joy to others, was now filled with ash. It had turned into an awful croak.

For almost twenty years now he'd walked the hollows and ridges and marsh prairies, speaking at church tent revivals, spreading truths, no matter how ugly, as he saw fit. Saving some, damning others, and forcing a great many to their most destructive sin and vice. He felt no remorse because he was only a vessel for God and God's madness.

And now the angels told him to come home again, because his daughter—*his very own daughter,* for he was the father who had set her course, because he could not kill her in the cradle—was about to give birth.

Hallelujah.

These were to be his acolytes and aides: two moonshine-running, gator-skinning, local backwood murderers, as beautiful as Lucifer and just as evil.

They had been pawns of their father, Farrell Ferris, who thirty years ago would beat Jester in the schoolyard every afternoon because Jester would eat lunch alone while reading the Bible. Farrell Ferris, his tormentor, had grown worse with age and moonshine.

The blood on his hands became thicker and redder until he was stained to the elbows. These boys had been fed that malevolence and had flourished on it.

He drew back the rage into himself and released the Ferris boys, who rolled in the mud and wept across the ripped clothes and makeup cases of Marcie Andrews. When they could move again, wincing in pain, they both stood and trembled in the heat, without any idea of what to do next.

"I knew your father," Jester said. "When I was a boy."

"He was the meanest critter this swamp hollow ever done seen," Duffy said.

"'Sides us, a'course," Deeter added.

"You made it last. The killing of him."

Duffy nodded, his mane of golden curls sprawling to his shoulders. "Took a while 'fore him and Mama finally done give up their ghosts. We wasn't very strong then, but we could still wield ax handles. Wouldn't have been much fun watchin' him die quick, now would it?"

"Hell no, where's the joy in that?" Deeter turned to Jester and said, "Last time he made to strike us we got out his own shotgun and blew off the big toe on his foot, then broke his arms some with the ax handles and chased him through the briar till he was so torn up that he looked like ... like ..." Deeter's hands moved in useless gestures. Try as he might, he could think of nothing that looked as raw as that.

"Like us after one'a his early-morning-to-mid-afternoon whippings."

"That's right, like us. And he was hung up in the brambles, caught on a thousand thistles, and we sat down before him with a jug of moon and watched him struggle and bleed to death from the scratches. Was a mighty jubilant sight, it was."

"It was," Duffy said, "a rapturous sight. Yes, it was."

Breathing in their hate and enjoying the heady scent of it, Brother Jester said, "After twenty years of preaching in the mountains and the valleys, I've come home again for a reason. God has set me on this path and finally allowed me to return to its beginning. I have need of you two. God is the master, I am merely the servant. And you are now servants to the servant."

Duffy and Deeter exchanged a panicky glance and nodded, biding their time.

"I lost my skinnin' knife," Duffy said. "Somewhere in the mud. I feel nekkid without it."

"You want, Reverend, we'll get you full up on some grits and gator meat."

"I don't share food with anyone."

"That much is plenty evident, Preacher!"

Jester smiled in the night, his teeth burning. "I eat only what is provided for me dead in the road. And I'm not a preacher anymore. Call me Brother Jester."

"What you come back here to Enigma for? What you gonna do? Why you among us again?"

"I've come for my daughter," Brother Jester said. "Sarah."

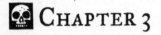# CHAPTER 3

Waldridge had a little black hat and a pair of white gloves that he wore whenever he drove the early model Packard town car. Seriously early, maybe a 1936, but kept in excellent repair, glossily waxed, and fine-tuned. Hellboy figured he could understand the guy's feistiness if they made him dress up like this every time he went out to the market for a carton of milk or a pack of cigarettes. The chauffeur uniform somehow matched the Packard, which despite its age still had some real horsepower to it. Hellboy sat in the enormous back seat, which was large enough to fit all six silent sisters, side by side.

"You drive the Nail ladies around much?" Hellboy asked.

"They ain't left the house in years. They used to love piling in back, having picnics down by the waterfalls, chasing butterflies and moths in the honeysuckle fields. Even after they was struck by evil intentions, they enjoyed goin' visitin' around town. They had friends, still had a chance for beaus and maybe even happiness. But that's all gone now. Bad will and corrupt notions have worn away at them. Was a time when Mr. Bliss Nail would ask the gospel singers, travelin' ministries, and faith healers to stop on up at the house, but no one could do nuthin' for them girls."

Waldridge caught Hellboy's eyes in the rearview and asked, "You really think you can help them or Miss Sarah?"

"I'm going to try."

"Tha's all a man can do, I s'pose."

As they crossed the town of Enigma, Hellboy gazed out the window at the quaint stores bordering both sides of a one-stoplight main street. The post office shared space with a bait and tackle shop. A dilapidated set of railroad tracks ran along a pumpkin patch and faded into greater disrepair in the distance. Decades had passed since this line had been used.

Small homes littered the area, almost swallowed by the landscape. Ancient, knobbed trees contorted and writhed in the breeze, the brush alive with some kind of action. He saw eyes glimmering high in the branches and he shifted in his seat.

"Sloths," Waldridge said. "You know about them?"

"Just as a sin."

That got a laugh out of the houseman. "Plenty of that around these parts too. If the corn liquor don't get 'em then their worst ambitions might."

Hellboy saw several trucks and horse-drawn carriages filled with men riding through town, many of the men apparently drunk.

"What are they doing?"

"They comin' in from the day's work."

"Where?"

"Where their daddies and grandaddies toiled in tomfoolery."

Hellboy figured that was the choice way of saying the men were returning from making their moonshine. He watched police cruisers coast by. It was a different way of life down here than the rest of the world.

Farmland and barnyards rolled out into the distant darkness, Enigma itself blurring back into the swamplands. From here the town appeared to be nearly surrounded by the jungles of slough.

As they drove down a large dirt road, a huge house came into view, every window lit. More than a dozen young women sat in rockers and swinging love seats on a whitewashed wraparound porch, feeding and burping babies. A reedy voice backed by twanging guitars drifted from a radio.

"We're there," Waldridge said. "I ain't got no business in that home so I'll wait for you right here in the car." He settled into the seat, dipped his hat over his eyes, and was snoring lightly before Hellboy turned away.

There was a lot of activity going on around Mrs. Hoopkins's Home for Unwed Wayward Teenage Mothers & Peanut Farm.

With a large wooden cross bouncing on a length of twine around her neck, Mrs. Hoopkins trundled around the place chasing unwed wayward teenage girls through the house and scooping up babies left and right.

She was a middle-aged lady of bodily contradictions. Thin but somehow squat. Short but containing a large presence. Frail but with corded muscle, full of strength and vitality. Her face showed serious mileage but was still quite pretty, almost girlish in a way.

It was eight-thirty and Mrs. Hoopkins meant for all the babies to be fed, bathed, and changed within the next fifteen minutes, and everyone else to be in bed and asleep by nine.

Her pink-tinted hair, tied up with a scarf, looked something like a feather duster on top of her head. Wearing an apron, corrective sneakers, and with her stockings rolled down to her ankles, one might snicker at the way she was dressed, but she exuded a kind of hard-earned class and was due respect. She took care of business, Mrs. Hoopkins did.

The large living room was thick with naugahyde, braided throw rugs, doilies, crocheted blankets, and paint-by-numbers Jesus, Elvis, and Conway Twitty. Mrs. Hoopkins looked at Hellboy and asked, "For the love of the sweet baby Jesus in the manger, you ain't gonna bring me no more misfortune into my house, are you?"

"No, ma'am," he answered.

"Well, praise the Almighty for that anyway. We got us enough troubles."

"Anything to do with Sarah—?" He realized then that he didn't know what her last name might be. Not Nail. "Ahh—nineteen, both her parents died about a year ago?"

"Only iffun you count that she's gone. Her and two other girls, they licked out sometime before dawn. Had the sheriff in and out of here all mornin', him and his deputies been searchin' all over town, but I fear. I fear."

"Where'd she go? Do you have any idea?"

"She's been actin' fidgety lately all right, but she in her ninth month and that happens every so often. Them other girls, Becky Sue Cabbot and Hortense—"

Hellboy thought, Hortense, ah jeez.

"—Millford, they both ready to drop their bundles too."

"Sheriff's here 'gin, Mrs. Hoopkins!" one of the girls called.

Mrs. Hoopkins said, "Well, he's a man of true conviction, I'll give him that."

Hellboy drew back a frilly curtain and watched as a police cruiser pulled up in front of the house and parked next to the Packard. The sheriff climbed out of the passenger side. Guy was hefty, carrying a lot of extra weight around the middle. He took off his hat and drew the back of his hand across his brow, took out a handkerchief, and daubed around his neck. Behind the wheel, his deputy settled deeper into the seat, dipped his hat over his eyes, and went to sleep. Hellboy was starting to see a theme here.

The sheriff liked to enter a room so everybody knew he was there. He clopped in through the front door loudly. "Whee-ah, sure is hot out there!"

Mrs. Hoopkins said, "You say that every night."

"'Cause every night it's hot!"

A solid tactic. You went in noisy and tried to shake everybody up, see what fell out, determine who scurried for cover. It focused attention. Hellboy stood back, and the sheriff smiled broadly at him.

"Sheriff Jebediah Hark, son, pleased to meet you."

"Sheriff," said Hellboy.

"Bliss Nail gave me a call about you. Said he hired you to help him out."

"He didn't hire me, but I am trying to help. What do you think happened to these girls?"

Scratching at his jowls with one hand, Sheriff Hark boosted up his gun belt with the other. Crimson-faced and drenched with sweat, he looked like he was hurtling toward a massive coronary. "Might be they left for their own for reasons we don't know about. Or maybe, well—it ain't happened for a spell, but in times past we seen a share of children being taken by the deep swamp folk."

"Taken?"

"Sometimes they sell the babies to rich families in Savannah and Athens or raise them as their own to toil on their farms out in the morass of their village. And then mayhap there's times when . . . well . . ."

Hellboy waited. "Well?"

"Children in these parts ain't always born, ah . . ."

"Ah?"

Mrs. Hoopkins said, "He means they're sometimes different. Got them some extra fingers or bodies covered with fur. Or no arms or too many arms, or they swim and crawl and slither but never walk."

"And the swamp folk take them in?" Hellboy asked.

"Tha's right."

"And the girls?"

"On occasion they come home again," the sheriff said, leaving the implication heavy in the air. "And sometimes they don't."

"So where is this village?"

"Ain't nobody rightly knows. We've had men who've gone out there lookin'. Some return ain't never seen it. A few, well, they says they seen it but most of them were outta their heads from fever and dehydration and maybe snakebite. Others, they've never been heard from again. Maybe gators got 'em, maybe sink holes. Maybe not."

He looked back at the sheriff and said, "Mrs. Hoopkins doesn't seem to think the girls were taken."

"That's what I say. They been having bad dreams and left on their own early this morning."

"They ain't anywhere in town," Sheriff Hark told her.

As an outsider, Hellboy found it especially difficult trying to dig through the layers of open secrets. Maybe the sheriff was just trying to be polite while talking about freaks face to face with Hellboy. He might be more worried about the swamp folk than he let on, or perhaps he wasn't worried at all and was trying to mislead Hellboy so they wouldn't trip over each other while investigating. No matter how fast you wanted to cut through the crap, it took some dancing around before you could do it.

Mrs. Hoopkins told the two men to sit and poured two glasses of milk. She handed them plates with slices of a dark purple pie on them. "Here, you boys have some briarberry."

It took Hellboy aback. He'd never heard of briarberry pie and the sound of it made his throat tighten.

Mrs. Hoopkins sat and said, "Them girls were havin' dreams, Jebediah."

"You keep saying that, to no disregard," Hark said, his mouth full. "But you still cain't tell me what kinda dreams they were."

"That Sarah, she's tryin' to keep ahead of some kind of evil that's been chasin' her in her nightmares. Every night for more than two weeks she'd been wakin' up in a froze sweat, weepin' and callin'."

"Callin' on who?"

"On that John Lament."

"That boy? I always liked him when he show up." Hark sipped some more milk and had a final forkful of pie. "But he ain't been around in more than a year, has he?"

"Not that I know," Mrs. Hoopkins said. "But he's a drifter, comes and goes as he pleases, and now her dreamin's caught on with some of the other girls."

"Becky Sue and Hortense," Hellboy said.

"That's right. They dreamed their babies would be born . . . *wrong.*"

"Ill children," the sheriff put in.

"Pumpkin-headed or pinheaded." She turned to Hellboy. "Now and then, well . . . sometimes the poison in the ground comes up and gets in the blood, or venom in the blood gets into the ground."

Mutants. Probably because of all the contaminated moonshine made out here over the last century, the outbreaks of yellow and scarlet fevers. And more recently due to the toxic waste dumped into the marshes by big corporations. Barrels of hazardous waste, perhaps even radioactive material, brought down in eighteen-wheeler caravans. Who the hell knew what might have been tossed out there to avoid federal regulations and health codes.

Mrs. Hoopkins said, "You ain't eatin', son. Why ain't you eatin' my pie?"

"Sorry, had a big dinner at Bliss Nail's house."

"Nobody in that house can cook the way I can."

"No, ma'am."

"Give it here," the sheriff said, pulling the plate to him and digging in.

Another toddler stepped into the kitchen and went for Hellboy's tail. Mrs. Hoopkins came flying out of her seat and shouted, "Lolly Mae, ain't you got a boy needs some changin' and feedin'?"

"Yes, ma'am."

"Well then, get him off that big fella's posterior and get on with it. We all got to pull our weight, and tomorrow gonna be a big day on the farm."

"Yes, ma'am."

Lolly Mae picked up her son, did a little curtsey, and raced upstairs.

Flailing her arms, Mrs. Hoopkins said, "These girls got to get them some rest. Those who can got's to harvest peanuts on the morrow."

Hellboy had seen a lot across the world, but he'd never seen anybody work a peanut farm before. He wished he had time to watch such a thing. "I understand."

The sheriff finished his other slice of pie, stood, and followed Hellboy to the door. "You wanna wait until morning and I'll send some men with you."

"I can't wait," Hellboy said.

"Then you be safe, son."

Mrs. Hoopkins pressed a hand atop his own. "You think you can find them three girls out there in the slough 'fore any danger befalls them?"

"I'm going to try."

"I got me a bad feeling in these old bones."

Hellboy thought, Me too, but said nothing.

Tapping at the driver's window, Hellboy waited while Waldridge snorted awake from his nap. He told the houseman that he was going to go off and look for the bog village.

"You want I should go with ya?"

"No, that's okay. I was just hoping you could point me in the right direction."

"You just gonna set off walkin'?"

"Yeah." He knew that something would be along to shove and prod him on the way. Ever since he'd been let off in Enigma he'd felt he was being watched.

"Swamp that way," Waldridge said, angling his index finger south-east down a dirt track. "They say it's eight hundred square miles. Heard it on the radio once."

Only about 450,000 acres. "That's not so bad."

"You don't know your way 'round these black waters."

"Do you?"

Waldridge considered the question. "No man does fully, but it's better to have someone with ya. In case'a ... well, snakebite ... and to keep an eye out for gators."

A tough old feisty dude, all right. Hellboy said, "Thanks anyway. I appreciate the offer, but there's things I'm better off doing alone."

"I s'pect you're right about that. Hope to meet up with you again soon. If not, you'll always have my prayers."

Hellboy knew what they were worth, but it was nice to hear anyway.

So he knocked.

The thin pineboard door of the dilapidated shanty slowly opened, answered by a hulk of a man who managed to tower even over Hellboy. The giant looked back over his shoulder and said, "Mama, Satan hisself is at the door."

"Then let him on in, Luther," an ancient, but oddly powerful voice, called. "'Fore he get up to any mischief out there."

"Come on in, O Lucifer, Son of the Morning!"

Well, Hellboy thought, this is going to be fun.

Lit from the glow of a blazing fire within, Luther's eyes burned a strange bronze. He stood nearly seven feet tall and went at least three hundred pounds of hard muscle. His enormous head was crowned by a small tuft of wispy yellow hair. In his left hand he held two dead rabbits, and hooked on his huge pinky was a jug of moonshine.

"Satan," Luther said, "don't stir no strife in this here house."

"Luther, if you don't start any crud with me, I won't with you. Deal?"

"I reckon that's as fair an offer as I'm likely to get from the Devil."

"Probably," Hellboy admitted. "At least today."

Luther moved aside and Hellboy stepped in, his upper lip curling in response to the overwhelming stink of cooked meat.

Tucked into her small wooden wheelchair a crone sat, smoking a corncob pipe. She was missing both legs, her left arm, right eye, and both ears. Long white hair grew in crazed clumps, some braided, some knotted into a pattern he recognized as a Litany Web. Powerful mojo.

Behind her, against a shack wall abundant with cracks stuffed full of mud and sawgrass, he saw numerous jars filled with amber fluid and dark floating matter. Labeled in a childlike scrawl were: Granny's Left Thumb, Granny's Right Big Toe, Granny's Shinbones, Luther's Wisdom Teeth, Boysenberry Jam, Granny's Anterior Margin of Pancreas, Granny's Celiac Ganglia with the Sympathetic Plexuses of the Abdominal Viscera, Luther's Kidney Stones, Peaches.

"I'm Granny Lewt," the woman said. "We got business together, you and me."

"We do?"

"Tha's right."

Drinking his moonshine, the hulking Luther tossed the rabbits onto a broad wooden kitchen table and began to skin them. He was very adept with the thick cutting blade, and Hellboy didn't want to think about what that might imply, considering the old woman's current state.

"Let me hear what's on your mind, lady."

"You showin' up like this only gonna make bad matters come together that much faster."

"Usually does."

"Ayup. You put fear into the things that ain't afraid'a much in this world or the next." She plucked out her pipe and pointed the end at Hellboy. "Wish there were more like you around."

"Be careful saying things like that," Hellboy said. "You never know who might be listening."

In the center of the stone hearth a black pot of stew bubbled. Luther gutted the rabbits, chopped the meat and some vegetables, several of which Hellboy didn't recognize, and threw it all into the cauldron. Some of the liquid boiled over and splashed the inside of the fireplace. The flames heaved. A heavy draft swept by, moaning and wheezing through the perforated walls and up the chimney.

"You heard tell'a Brother Jester?" Granny Lewt asked.

"Yeah, him I heard about already. Can I go now?"

"Don't you shrug that one off too lightly."

Holding onto the pipe with her remaining two fingers, Granny Lewt snaked her right hand—her only hand—through the air for emphasis. Then she sat back and puffed deeply, enjoying her smoke.

The old woman said, "He's out there in Enigma right now. I don't know his meaning. He's got power, and he's sly."

"They all are. Don't worry about me, I've been doing this a long time."

"I pray tell that's so. But you don't know these swamps, and these here black waters is different than anything you ever known before."

He'd been in Jerusalem when the Whore of Babylon crept out of the olive trees at the Garden of Gethsemane. He'd fought off goblins and trolls and African tribal demons that possessed snakes sixty feet long. He'd gone head to head with the Japanese Lord of War called Aragami, the fury of wild violence, the God of Battle, slayer of 8,888 men, and Hellboy had trounced him. He hadn't been so damn tough.

So Hellboy figured that a little moss and slime, a few thorny patches and a lot of mud, some guy who took his troubles out on a bunch of girls . . . well, he could handle it.

Granny Lewt said, "There's someone else out there you gotta watch out for."

"There always is," Hellboy sighed. "Would that be this Lament character?"

As she nodded, Granny's blanket slid from around her shoulders and he saw the clean edge of scar tissue to her amputated arm. "He got power, that boy, but he been away in the world a long time. He used to preach the gospel in a golden voice dazzling as the rising sun. But I don't know which side'a this thing he likely to come down upon. He got a history with the walking darkness, he does."

Hellboy wondered why anybody ever tried to give him advice when, in the end, nobody knew a goddamn thing anyway.

"You know where this village is supposed to be?"

"Nobody knows except them that's got to know."

"Well, that's helpful. So, any idea where I should start?"

"You walk southeast to the bottoms," Granny said. "Follow the road, bear to the left. You'll find a skiff and stobpole there."

"A what and a what?"

"A boat and a pole to push it yonder into the sweet blackwater." Granny Lewt appraised him and said, "For a worldly—for a beyond the worldly—big critter like you, you ain't so well-versed in our ways."

"Lady, this place isn't all that special except it's a lot greener and more humid than most." He peered into her withered face, as deep as he figured he could go, and asked, "You think those girls and their babies will be all right?"

"I pray so, but there ain't no way to know until it's their time for the chillun to come out in the world. I tell you this though, that Brother Jester get to whisperin' at 'em, or he toss out a shadow upon 'em, he gonna cuss 'em fer sure. They be born in some bad way. There's a thousand years'a half-gnawed bones hidden in them briar patches and under that morass. You go in alone with no guide, you ain't gonna ever come home again."

"You people are starting to freak me out a little," Hellboy admitted. "How about if you save the creepy speeches for the next guy who comes down the road and just let me get on with it?"

"I'd tell you to wait until mornin'—a lotta men been lost in that slough at high noon, much less at night—but we both know the minutes is melting away like a slivered candlestick. You gonna need somethin' to help you on your way."

She rooted around in her blankets for a moment and he expected her to come up with a charm or amulet, the way the witches usually did. But instead she just got out a pouch of tobacco and started to clean and refill her pipe with her one hand. Her wrinkled, liver-spotted fingers were still extremely nimble. She tamped the tobacco in, stuck the pipe between her teeth again, lit a match against the underside of her chair, and set to smoking once more. Hellboy waited.

Granny Lewt wheeled herself to the fire and filled a wooden bowl of stew. It steamed and hissed and popped, and Hellboy wondered how anybody could eat such a meal. He was hungry and started to wonder if he was ever going to get any edible chow this side of the Mason–Dixon line.

"Here," she said, "have some supper."

"Thanks anyway."

"You gotta eat it."

"What do you mean?"

"You gotta get some into you so's you can git about in the bog with my eyes and ears." She placed it on her lap and rutted about for a spoon. Stuck it in the bowl and proffered it to him.

He blinked at her. "Your eyes and ears?"

"It'll help you in your hour of need."

"Lady, the only need I've got right now is to get the hell out of here."

"Listen up now, boy, Granny Lewt been around these parts a lot longer than you. I's one of the three sisters of the swamp and I's here to help as much as I can, and help you's what I'm'a gonna do. We bound, we three sisters. We can only do so much. So let me do what I needs to."

"Look, I appreciate the effort, but I'm going now."

"You cain't!"

Hellboy turned and went for the door, and of course it was gone.

"Ah nuts to this." He lifted his fist to pound through the wall and Luther grabbed him by the wrist and held on tightly.

"Hey! I told you not to start any crap with me!"

"Granny say you gotta eat!"

"Back off, pal!"

But the massive brute wasn't about to listen to reason, and he didn't seem to have the IQ points to figure out not to mess with big red badasses, so Hellboy did his best to shove the lumbering guy away without hurting him.

But Luther had some real strength to him, beyond anything Hellboy was expecting. Soon he realized he couldn't hold back, and they really started to brawl.

"Here," Granny Lewt said, holding the bowl out to her son. The giant was able to continue fighting even while he reached for the stew, the jug of moonshine still hanging off his pinky. "He ain't got his mind quite right yet. We got's to help him."

"Iffun you say so, Mama."

"He got hisself some misery a'comin' already. Don't hurt him none, Luther."

"Iffun you say, Mama."

Like he didn't have enough to put up with already, Hellboy had to listen to them talk about him like he wasn't even in the room.

Luther moved in quickly, low, growling like an animal now.

"Last chance here, pal. I spend all my time smashing down things bigger and uglier than me. I'd say I've got this one in hand. I'm warning you."

"Mister Satan, jest do what Mama say and I won't have to hit you no more."

You had to give it to him, this backwoods swamp rat certainly was a single-minded true believer.

Hellboy hauled off and slapped Luther in the head with his stone hand. Luther let out a yelp and almost went down to one knee. Almost. Then he stood to his full height, cocked the jug over his shoulder to his lips, sucked down some moon, wiped his mouth with the same hand, held the bowl out before him, and moved forward again.

You couldn't just lie down and let them walk over you, jamming rabbit bits and eyeballs and pancreases down your maw. Sometimes you had to take a stand against even the people who were trying to help.

Granny continued smoking calmly, watching the fray.

Hellboy hauled off and threw a roundhouse at the giant Luther, who moved into the blow with incredible speed, allowing himself to be struck. The force of impact made the walls creak and murmur, the flames rising much higher in the hearth. The old woman's wheelchair rolled across the room backward and almost crashed into the wall. She gripped a wheel and spun in circles, cackling and whooping wildly, enjoying herself.

Shelves rattled savagely, and one jar tipped and rang against another before falling to the floor.

"You done set free my kidney stones!" Luther cried, and hurled himself at Hellboy once again.

This was just unbelievable. Hellboy started to buckle and barely managed to stay on his feet. Granny Lewt blew out a stream of smoke and said, "Ya cain't win because you ain't fightin' evil this time. In your heart you know we's your friends, and what's got to happen is what's got to be."

"Son of a—!"

In the midst of his curse, wondering if the old lady was some-how right, Hellboy's eyes grew wide as Luther slung forward the bowl of stew and slopped it into his mouth. Oh Jesus. You could put up with a lot but really, having an old woman's eyes and ears and maybe her Celiac Ganglia with the Sympathetic Plexuses of the Abdominal Viscera washing down your throat, it was just too much. His stomach tumbled and he gritted his teeth, about to launch himself at Luther and finish this fiasco, when the giant moved away and began cleaning up the broken shards of glass, col-lecting his kidney stones.

"It's done," Granny Lewt said. "You got my eyes and ears now. Wonders to behold, swamp songs to hear tell, and a little more protection."

"Ugh, Jesus Christ!" Hellboy doubled over, spitting and wip-ing his mouth with the tail of his overcoat. "You people are god-damn nuts!"

The door was back. Hellboy tore it open and rushed into the swamp outside, the water and muck almost to his knees, and heard Luther say, "Don't worry none, Mr. Satan, I ain't really mad at ya 'bout my kidney stones. You come on back and we'll share a jug soon."

As Hellboy watched, the shack began retreating into the darkness, the mud and brambles and slimy water drawing away with it, until nothing but dark brush and the distant marsh prairies surrounded him, and he was back on the dirt road.

Now he had to follow it, see if he could find Sarah and the others out there in the glowing green night.

He started along and heard a car coming. He turned and the world quickly brightened around him until he was blinded. He threw his hand up in front of his face as high-beam headlights burst against him like white molten metal. Doing better than seventy, a Dodge Charger came bearing down on him like the wrath of Hell.

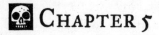# CHAPTER 5

The Charger roared down on one hell of an ugly sight that had suddenly appeared right there in the middle of the road.

Duffy Ferris rose up in his seat and let out a gruesome giggle. He couldn't help himself, murder was all he knew. He smiled broadly and stomped the pedal, aiming the center of the grille for the big red fella right there in front of him. The distance between them was chewed down to almost nothing, the fella's confused face and really big hand waving into the brights.

Lunging forward from the back seat, Brother Jester gripped the wheel from Duffy's hands and viciously tugged it aside. Deeter said, "Hey now, wha—?" as the three of them jounced wildly inside the car.

The suspension had been reinforced for hauling boxes of moonshine over mud flats and down across the bottoms. Welded iron plating protected the undercarriage as the Charger slid across thick brush on the side of the track. The car veered to the farthest edge of the shoulder and nearly over the rim of a ditch, the rear right tire slewing and strewing gravel. They lost a hubcap and it took Duffy another moment to regain control of the car.

"Now what'd you go and do a fool thing like that for, Preacher?" he asked. "If we'd run him over you coulda at least ate him." He sought out the reverend in the rearview, but could see nothing but darkness behind him.

Jester's black angels surrounded him, whispering secrets of

what had been and what might yet be. They hissed and he hissed, a new element added to his ruined voice. Maybe it was alarm or perhaps even fear. "Striking him would've only damaged your car, and I need to set out and find my daughter this night. Keep going."

"I ain't never seen that big ole boy 'round these parts before."

"Must be one of them swamp folk. He look like he drunk a jug or two of bad moon when he was a young'un."

Fading into the shadows that were not his own, Jester said, "He is fated to join my enemy and to become my enemy."

"Then why don't we pull over and take care of him?" Deeter asked.

"It's not the proper time."

"You gonna let us know when it is said proper time?"

"Oh yes, I surely will."

"Well, that's somethin' then. Where's she at? This daughter'a yours."

"She's pregnant and unwed, and alone for the moment."

"She ain't got no man?"

"She does, but he is not with her. She's alone."

"Mrs. Hoopkins's Home for Unwed Wayward Teenage Mothers & Peanut Farm," the Ferris boys said in unison.

The brothers knew where girls went when they had no family, money, or husband. In fact, they'd sent plenty of girls there themselves, and had a number of children littering the backwoods all over Enigma. Jester's shadows offered up names and faces that he swept aside with a turn of his head.

His mind filled with a single searing image—that of his daughter in her cradle, with her dead mother on the floor beside her in a pond of lapping blood.

"How far are we from this farm?" he asked.

"We nearly there," Duffy responded, still a touch angry about losing that hubcap. "You like peanuts?"

• • •

The Ferris boys and the dark preacher stood out on the front porch of Mrs. Hoopkins's place listening to the occasional sound of a crying child upstairs in the house. Mrs. Hoopkins smiled out her screen door at the Ferris brothers and said, "You handsome fellas here to visit any of your children?"

"Not right this evening, ma'am," Duffy told her, giving her a thousand-volt smile. It didn't quite work on her the way it did teenage girls, but the woman's stern features visibly softened.

"Well, what do you boys want here then?"

"Mrs. Hoopkins," Deeter said, "this here is Brother Jester, the famous minister who's traveled all around the Appalachians for near two decades spreading the good word. He's come back to Enigma to visit relations."

She peered at Jester for a moment and said, "I know you?"

"No, dear lady," he said, because he always spoke the truth, and she did not know him. No one did anymore, perhaps not even himself. The man she'd seen decades ago praising the Almighty in tents out in the cane fields was long gone.

"Lord above, you had a doctor look down that throat a'yours?"

"I am beyond curing."

"Nothing beyond the healing power of our savior Jesus Christ."

Jester smiled, showing yellow shards of teeth. And thinking, Oh but some things are, they are. We who are trapped by the will of God and His greater plans, those of us who are not meant to be healed, but have a more tragic part to play. Like Cain, Judas, and Pilate, like Lucifer and his minions. Creations of a Lord gone mad. Playing out the damning roles given to them. Created by Heaven but with more than a small touch of Hell to them.

"I smell fresh pie?" Deeter asked.

"That briarberry?" Duffy said. "Such a sweet aroma, my tongue done gone wet and wagging."

Mrs. Hoopkins showed her dentures and primped her pink hair with one hand, feeling the scarf still atop her head and untying it to let large looping curls flop loose like strands of baling wire. "You boys like a slice of pie and some milk?"

"We sure would," the Ferris brothers said in unison.

"You like a slice too, Reverend?"

"No," Jester said, "thank you."

"You look as if you could use a good home-cooked meal. Let me fix you somethin'."

"My spirit is sated, and thus so is my body. My rage sustains me."

"Whassat?"

"He says," Duffy said, "his faith 'stains him."

"Oh."

She got out the pie and set down plates, took a large cutting knife and sliced the Ferris boys two pieces. Turning to the refrigerator, she found there was more than a quart of milk still left. She poured two large glasses of milk and set them before the brothers, enjoying the intensity, the near-savagery with which they ate. She didn't notice that her cutting blade was no longer on the table.

Mrs. Hoopkins asked, "So why you gentlemen come visitin' at this hour? It's near nine-thirty. My girls and their babies need their sleep. We got harvestin' on the morrow."

"My dear woman," Brother Jester said. "I have inquiries into the whereabouts of one of the young women in your care. Sarah."

Pulling a pink ringlet from out of her eyes, frowning a bit, she began to speak and then curbed herself. She cocked her head and heard the children upstairs, so many of them crying when they'd been soothed and sleeping just minutes ago. After a moment of peering deeply at the preacher she said, "There's four Sarahs here, which one you got iniquities about?"

Jester was suddenly startled by the fact that he did not know the name of the family that had raised her. Bliss Nail had hidden her from him. The shadows seemed upset and flowed about inside him, knowing a mistake had been made but unsure of what to do about it. They moved toward the old woman but her strength of mind and resolve seemed to step before them and block their passage to the truth.

"She is nineteen," Jester said.

"There's three Sarahs here that age."

"Then I'll see all three of them now."

"But you won't, it's nigh unto nine thirty-five, and in this house we rise early."

"I can certainly understand your trepidation, but—"

"I don't allow my girls to linger with strangers out here in my kitchen this deep in the night. You got questions, visit during regular hours, just after supper time. We'll be havin' fried bluegill and hushpuppies tomorrow, and you're welcome to share."

"Tater hushpuppies!" Deeter said. "Ain't had them in many a hot summer!"

Jester glowered at the interruption and faced Mrs. Hoopkins again. "I thank you for that, dear woman, but I beg you to make a special consideration for me, in this case."

"And why'm I gonna do that?"

"The circumstances are exceptional."

An infant began to shriek upstairs and Brother Jester's heart both soared and cracked at the sound. He saw the hatchet covered in blood again, and could feel the rope tightening around his throat. The angel of death embracing his body in its freezing arms. He started to tremble, the power rising within him.

In an instant, he began to cry black tears, the motes of energy sparking and floating from him. Mrs. Hoopkins nearly fell over in her chair and Duffy reached over and pressed a hand to her back, holding her in place. Jester started to grin, his teeth fiery, and said, "Because if we don't go outside right this minute and I don't get the information I want, I'll have to drag you upstairs and slay all the girls and their children until I find my daughter. Sarah. Who is pregnant and who is nineteen."

"Lord have mercy," Mrs. Hoopkins whimpered.

"He does," Brother Jester said, "but not for me, and not for you this night."

Ushered outside, Mrs. Hoopkins spoke quickly but with a quiet innate strength. Even now, with the Ferris boys bracketing her in the yard, the lights of the house seeming so far away, with her death at hand, she stood with bold assurance. The shadows could hear her prayers in the back of her mind. With Brother Jester's eyes searing into her heart, she showed no fear at all for herself, but only for the girls and children in her care.

Jester loved the woman as much as he was able, despite what would have to happen next. He wanted to hug her to him and preach words of solace, even kiss her brow. He began petitioning Heaven as he turned away, gesturing for Duffy to put an end to it now.

In Duffy's hand, raised high, was her cutting knife, the edge still covered with briarberry and crumbs. She didn't make a sound as Brother Jester, once again alive with his own death, fell to his knees and began to weep black flame.

After they buried Mrs. Hoopkins out in the peanut patch, Deeter asked, "So who is this big ole red boy anyway?"

"A creature of both light and darkness who chooses not to know himself," Jester said. "Like me."

They would have to go out into the swamps and revisit his past. Not only to regain his daughter, heavy with his grandchild, but also to face his newfound brother-enemy caught in the same web between Heaven, earth, and Hell. Perhaps, Jester thought, they might redeem themselves together.

He let out a mangled stream of laughter from his ruined throat, filled with sorrow and madness.

The Ferris boys looked at each other, cruel men with dried blood beneath their fingernails, doing their best not to tremble in the humid darkness, and failing.

# CHAPTER 6

Hellboy had to give credit where it was due. The old lady's eyes seemed to be working just fine.

He could see pretty clearly in the night and he immediately recognized the lengthy stobpole standing in the skiff even though he'd never seen or used one before. A comforting knowledge and familiarity with the swamp engulfed him, as he walked through the ragged cypress, tupelo, sycamore stumps, and watergrass.

He spotted a skink in the branches above him. He didn't know what a skink was. Even now, staring at the thing, he didn't know what it was. But thanks to Granny Lewt, he knew it was a skink. Weird feeling.

A lantern hung on an iron brace at the back of the skiff. He reached into his belt and pulled out his Zippo lighter, lit the wick of the oil lamp, and enjoyed the warm glow it cast across the emerald hell.

He saw a paddle tied into some netting in the aft. He climbed into the skiff and shoved off, using the stobpole to brace and push free from the bottom of the slimy shallows. His movements had a strange grace that wasn't his own. All things being equal, he'd rather have tried it himself without having to eat that damn stew, but at least Granny Lewt's spell made this part of the journey easier.

Darkness somehow came alive with the infinite depths of green, eternal and brooding. He moved in a southeastern course, stobbing through the silent, shadow-strewn slough. The black waters were stagnant and mosquito-heavy, and overhead long vines and thick Spanish moss hung down from branches, fluttering in the slight hot breeze.

The keel bumped a log half-hidden in the weeds and spooked a limpkin awake. The ungainly bird hopped through the shallows using its stork-like legs to limp through the slime, its bill thick with bugs and snails. Its mouth opened and it let out a bizarre cry that carried through the bog, causing a low moaning caterwaul from nocturnal animals in the trees and tussocks all around. A loon's shriek tore through the night. Granny's ears were doing their job too.

Hellboy continued on, almost enjoying the repetitive motion of stobbing the boat, cutting cleanly through the water. Luna moths and mosquitos congregated around the lantern, the tinny hum loud in his head.

It went on like that for hours, until the moon was high overhead. The whole time he was uncertain he was moving in the right direction, or in any direction at all. There were no clues to follow in this place, no signs that anyone had been here over the last ten thousand years. He almost made to shout into the darkness, see if the girls might answer him from the depths of the brush. But who knew what that might arouse.

The yellow illumination from the lantern lit the right-hand bank as the waterway thinned and he came around a knoll of mud, root, and bramble. He heard something hit the water, flat and heavy. Then there was aggressive action in the shallows for a minute before a lulling silence, and his new ears told him that gators were on the move.

The canal narrowed to a swollen inlet which led to a far off dead-still lake, the banks rising and falling away into a black morass thick with tupelo, titi, and scrub oak. Billowing cypress towered above, casting a greater green glow across the landscape. Hellboy lifted the stobpole inboard and scanned the area. He saw figures converging on him, the ridged, wide-eyed, flat reptile heads coursing toward him.

He drew the lantern off its iron hinge and held it up, seeing more gators on the banks scrambling around in the mud on squat, disproportionate legs, hissing and snapping their long jaws. Ducks took off flapping into the dark and cat squirrels chittered up strangler-fig vines. He brought the back of his hand to his nose as a noxious smell assaulted him. The lantern flame flared and singed his fingers. He snapped it back onto its hook. There must be pockets of methane trapped in the bottoms around here.

Maybe it was time to talk. He said, "Hey now, boys, listen—"

A powerful thud rocked the skiff and nearly knocked him off his feet. Louder grunting and hissing made him turn and look behind him. The boat spun and drifted into deeper water. He grabbed up the stobpole once more and swept it out to batter the gators away. It splintered in his hands and he thought, Damn stupid move, I needed that thing.

Now he was stuck with no way back toward the bank. He tore at the netting and removed the oars, which looked small and ineffectual now. He slotted them in and tried rowing but didn't get far before he heard claws scrape across the bottom of the skiff. It pitched again, and a huge, powerful tail slammed into the bow, raising waves that splashed against his chest.

Hellboy had just enough time to say, "Son of a—" before the skiff flipped, hurling him into the brackish, gator-infested waters.

The emerald-black depths yawned wide even as other jaws tore at him. Tumbling over, something got hold of his ankle almost daintily and he was yanked down. He swung his fists and connected with thick reptilian scales, but without any leverage he wasn't doing much good. The gators twisted across his body and snapped at him, their claws shredding his overcoat and ripping at his belly.

He fought to swallow his shouts and pain, keeping his mouth tightly closed against the cold slimy slough. He got his stone hand up in front of his face and a pair of jaws locked on his wrist, yanking him forward. The tatters of his coat flapped up across his throat and he was jerked in another direction by his hoof, two gators tussling over him and playing tug-of-war for their dinner.

Granny Lewt was trying to tell him something. Jaws snapped shut on his upper leg and pulled him away from the others. He opened his mouth to let out a drowning warble. He could taste his own blood in the water. The churning froth of sludge erupted into his face and he became completely disoriented again. He hauled off, hammering with his fist, and managed to break the gator's grip. He lashed out with his tail, connecting with something. Okay, enough of this. He needed air. He tried to swim but wasn't sure he was heading to the surface. His instincts kept pushing Granny away, and with his brain burning from lack of oxygen he forced himself to settle down enough to hear whatever she needed him to hear.

Gators drag you down to their mud-holes, roll you under logs, and leave you rotting, sometimes in air pockets, fer days. They liked their meals tender. There were rumors of men who woke up with their feet chewed off, in the black twenty feet down, who had to dig their way back to the water before the bull gators came back to finish their supper.

They were pulling him down to a mostly submerged tussock island, where they could bury him in the roots. He had to move in the opposite direction and get to air. His brain was already getting foggy, his head full of white and red spatters.

Hellboy swung around hard and connected squarely with one of the gators. Felt like it was directly on its snout. He kicked hard then, feeling teeth snap off in the flesh of his ankle, and let loose with a cry that released the last of his air. A burst of bubbles tickled his forehead, and he knew which way was up.

He broke the surface spitting out Christ knew what, the thick sludge of swamp boiling around him. Oil from the broken lantern burned across the water and gave him a little light.

During the struggle he must've knocked the skiff aside. He saw it was overturned and stuck in a snarl of cypress roots not too far away. He swam for it. Behind him the bull gators had made it to the far bank of the inlet and were nursing their wounds.

Hellboy could touch bottom now but he kept slipping in the slime and flopping over on his face, unable to catch his breath. It was difficult going but he finally managed to shrug out of his ruined overcoat and get a hand on the boat.

Breathing heavily, he grabbed hold and took a step up the bank before he realized there was a hole in the bottom of the skiff. Not huge but big enough that he couldn't fix it. He let out a grunt of frustration and slid off-balance in the muck again. The skiff spun out of his reach, righted itself, and immediately started to sink. He turned away and found he was going under again.

He came up gagging and sucking wind. By the time he got ready to try and climb up from the shallows again, he heard the sharp sounds of hissing nearby.

"Terrific," he said. Two more bull gators were coming straight for him down the silt bank, their eyes shining with silver moonlight.

He thought about going for his gun but the possibility of bigger pockets of methane worried him. Dumb to die out here rolled to the bottom of some mud-hole, but it would be even worse if he blew himself up.

He said, "I'm not good eating, guys. Just go ask your other pals. Why don't you both just—"

The first bull slued forward, opening its jaws wide. Instead of waiting, Hellboy lunged, shifted his weight, and more or less fell directly across its nose. The gator scrambled along up the bank with Hellboy on its back. Good, they were getting to drier, firmer ground. Hellboy rolled off and stood in a crouch. After those hours in the skiff and slipping around in the mire, it was nice to have earth beneath his hooves again. When the bull turned to make another pass he caught hold of its tail and held on. The second gator tried to go for his legs, but Hellboy hauled its brother around, lifted it high, and brought it slamming down on the other's back in a crushing blow of muscle and scale. While they tried to untangle themselves, Hellboy grabbed what was left of his coat, put it back on, and moved further along the narrow shore.

In the distance he saw flame.

The mud bank thinned until he was back in the water. Forced to swim and crawl through the morass, clambering across sand-banks and tussocks of briar, thorn, and barb, he made his way toward the fire.

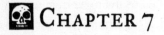# CHAPTER 7

The dark lake glistened with star shine, the rim of the water a searing white as if slabs of light had been laid end to end around its edge.

It took him over an hour to reach the camp, and by the time he got there he was exhausted, half-drowned, completely covered in mud and rotting vegetation, and he was sick to his stomach from swallowing so much swamp water. Or maybe it was the old lady's Celiac Ganglia with the Sympathetic Plexuses of the Abdominal Viscera, but he really didn't want to think about that.

A skiff had been beached in white sand, and nearby a young man sat playing a mouth-harp. The guy had a campfire going with something freshly killed cooking on a spit. Thankfully the old lady hadn't given Hellboy her nose too. He didn't want to know what it was he was watching sizzle in the flames.

He figured this had to be John Lament. A deep calm seemed to settle around and within the guy. He was maybe twenty-five, but with a shock of white right up front in his otherwise wavy brown hair. Dressed in jeans, suspenders, and a light white linen shirt rolled up to the middle of his muscular forearms.

Lament quit his twanging, looked up, and said, "Well son, you look like you've had a hell of a time of it out in these black waters." He drew a blanket from a rucksack. "Dry off and come sit by the fire 'fore you catch your death."

Hellboy nodded his thanks, yanked off his belt and ragged coat, and dried himself, doing his best to clean off the mud. His ankle was chewed up pretty bad and he had deep lacerations across his thigh. He tore off a couple of lengthy strips from his coat and bound his wounds, then put his belt back on.

Lament offered a small jug. "You want a tap of moon to kill the pain?"

Might as well make sure he was dealing with the right person. "You're Lament?"

"Yessir. John Lament. Pleased to make your acquaintance."

Lament made as if to shake hands. Hellboy held out his right fist. Lament's face broke into a wide grin. Hellboy put his hand down.

As good a time as any to get the ball rolling. Hellboy opened a compartment on his belt and tossed the Dome of the Rock charm, expecting some real action this time. Lament caught it in his left hand, turned the medallion over, and checked the ancient inscription.

His lips quivered as if he was fighting to frame unfamiliar words. Then he said, *"'I invoke the protection of the Green One, Tamuz, Aradia, and Anu-Sais. I command evil and death to disperse and the moon to appear in my hand.'"*

That got Hellboy's notice. He scratched between the stubs of his horns. "You read Sumerian?"

"No," Lament told him, "but it speaks to me. You go 'round throwin' this thing at every stranger you run across?"

"Lately," Hellboy admitted, "it seems that I have."

"Not very civilized."

Lament threw the charm back and Hellboy pocketed it once again. The old lady had been right. The swamps were like nowhere else he'd ever visited.

"Listen," Hellboy said as Lament twanged another tune. "I've had a kind of bad day so far. So if you want to rumble let's do it now and get it out of the way."

Lament quit picking at his mouth-harp and looked up. "Rumble?"

"Fight."

"Why we gonna do a foolish thing like that?"

"I didn't say we should, I just said if you wanted to I'd oblige you."

"Right neighborly that is." Sitting up, Lament checked the meat on the spit. "You hungry?"

Hellboy said, "Considering I just drank half the damn swamp, and before that I got a spoonful of a granny witch's stew jammed down my throat, and before that a big catfish stared at me like he'd scream if I stuck a fork in him, I don't think I'll ever be hungry again."

That got Lament chuckling. It was an easy, honest laughter. He lifted his chin and squinted at Hellboy. "Yep, now I recognize them eyes. You been suppin' with Granny Lewt tonight. She's a right fine lady but her manners could use some polish. She did what she done to help you, so be at ease about the rest of it." He tapped the meat on the spit with a stick and said, "No worries 'bout this food right here."

"What is it?"

"Gray squirrel."

Hellboy turned aside in disgust. "I think I'll pass anyway."

"Iffun you say."

Lament ate the meat directly off the spit, tearing at it with his teeth and occasionally drinking from his jug. He kind of hummed and sang as he ate, fully enjoying his meal. Hellboy watched, a little dismayed. He'd been edgy and waiting for a fight, and the ruckus with the gators hadn't gotten the tension out of his system yet. The smell of his own drying blood made him anxious, and his tail kept twitching at mosquitoes.

Stepping up, he loomed over Lament and decided to brace him. "What are you doing out here?"

Swallowing a bite of food, Lament said, "Same thing as you, I reckon."

"You have no idea what I'm about."

"That ain't rightly true, son."

"How about if you lay it on the line? You people talk pretty but you take up a lot of air before you actually get around to saying anything much. I'm in a hurry."

"Are you?"

Thinking about the time he'd killed on his way down south, hitching and brooding, alone with his thoughts and his bad mood, Hellboy realized he hadn't been in a rush to do much of anything. It had been okay to put all the miles behind him, wet in the rain. But now it was different. There were teenage girls lost out there, and he wanted to make certain they were safe before he called it a day.

"Yeah," he said. "I am. So how about you answer my question. What are you doing out here?"

"I did answer. You just ain't in the mind to hear."

Lament finished the meat on the spit and threw the remainder into the fire. He lifted his mouth-harp to his lips and played a bit more, somehow making the song sound pretty. Hellboy wouldn't have thought it possible, strumming a rubber band and making music.

When Lament finished he sighed hard enough to fan the fire. "I'm here to save my Sarah from harm, and them other girls swole with children too. Same as you, ain't that the case? 'Cept none of this is your burden."

"You need help, so I'm here."

"Well, if you're of a like mind and want in with my task and purpose, I could use a friend. You want out, I can point you the way any time you like. Fair 'nuff?"

Hellboy decided it was. "Fair enough." He sat at the fire and looked around, then spotted a rucksack. "I don't suppose you have a candy bar or a bag of pretzels you could share, now do you?"

"Caught some catfish earlier, if you want a taste."

Hellboy grimaced. "Christ, not with the catfish again."

Bull gators roared in the distance, the loons cried into the night. Reflections from a dozen peering eyes made Hellboy turn and turn again. The tension rose within him once more and the muscles in his back tightened. "Shouldn't we keep going, make sure Sarah and the others are all right out there?"

Lament said, "There ain't a critter anywhere in this swamp that can get the drop on her. She been out in these marsh prairies since she was baptized. In fact, it happened right here, on this basin. The holy spirit visitin' her."

"How do you know?"

"How do you think, son? Because I was there." He then pointed to a patch of flattened weeds and a few strewn rocks nearby. "They made camp here a day or so ago."

"For someone who claims he wants to save those girls, you don't seem too worried about them."

"I am," Lament said. "But it's a loser's game to stumble about in the dark on the blackwater."

Hellboy thought, Did he just call me a loser? "Hey, pal—"

"You already shovin' your luck just by not already bein' gator bait. You travel any farther at night and ain't nobody ever gonna see your princely face again. Like I said, Sarah knows these waters better than damn near anybody in Enigma. The man who raised her wrassled gators out in these parts, and used to head up the swamp tent revivals and the all-night gospel sings."

"You're from here."

"I been adrift all over."

"But you know Enigma."

"I know Enigma."

"There's someone else after her. Sarah and the girls."

"Ayup."

"You know him?"

"I know him."

"What if that guy doesn't camp tonight?"

"Then he'll probably be knockin' on the pearly gates by mornin' and we won't have to worry about it 't'all. Sometimes, problems have a way of rightin' themselves." He gestured vaguely. "There's a swamp shanty town yonder. We'll make for it come sunup."

"You know where it is?"

"You sure are a curious fella, ain't ya. I know where it is."

"Where's yonder?"

"Well, when we find it we'll know for sure. Now, lay in on that blanket and let's get some sleep."

Hellboy laid down. He wasn't sure that he could trust this guy, and said, "I'm not sure I can trust you."

But Lament merely turned away from the fire, drew his blanket over his shoulder, and soon was softly snoring.

It had been a hell of a day all right.

As Hellboy fell asleep he saw the shadows lengthening, thickening around the campsite, easing toward him to clutch at his clothes and face. They spoke in an infantile and inhuman language that he couldn't name but could still understand. They told him he would find remorse and pain in the marsh, but he should be true to his own secret heart. He brushed the shadows from his nose as he settled in to dream, hearing the children calling him.

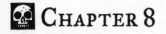 CHAPTER 8

Jester sat in shadow with the demon's secrets.

It had been too late to take a skiff into the swamp, with the moon already beginning to rise, so they'd decided to wait until sunup. The Ferris boys lived in a two-room shack not far from the house where Brother Jester had been raised by his own brutal father, another man corrupted by bitterness, ignorance, and corn liquor. They were terrified that Jester would murder them in their sleep, and they tried to appease him any way they could. They offered him food, wine, and the tramp down the lane, and even their sagging, fetid mattresses although Jester hadn't slept under a roof in twenty years.

Jester hadn't slept in twenty years. His mind periodically wandered away from his body, and the body occasionally rested.

They gave him a torn blanket spattered with old bloodstains. It was a child's blanket and featured a cartoon bird character. He folded it and laid it on their sagging back-porch step and sat there looking into the lush vegetation of the woodland that eventually cascaded into the marshes.

Held within the folds of their black wings, the shadows of angels brought with them the secrets of the sleeping demon, aflame with hellfire. When the shadows dropped the mysteries, puzzles, and contradictions at Jester's feet, the dark preacher poked through them with the toe of his shoe, struggling but incapable of understanding.

A Russian who would not die. A loving foster father, a hard man of justice. A once-evil but eventually repentant mother. A prince of Sheol. Enormous unholy beasts with the faces of pigs, frogs, and dogs. Brutish shamblers that burned from the touch of iron or innocence. Griddle cakes. Horseshoes. Holy water and the bones of saints.

Brother Jester took off his hat, cleaned the brim with his hand-kerchief, and put it back on.

Children. Inhuman, horrific in nature, but blessed. Calling to God and those that aid God's will. And the Holy Spirit giving favor.

A great tree of life, perhaps the very tree of knowledge still bearing fruit in the garden of Eden, away from mankind's trans-gressions.

Those were only the few images he could easily grasp. A great-er number of them were visions and scraps of infernal knowledge that tore into his mind. They went behind his small human brain and settled at the back of his skull where his immortal rage sat perched, waiting to eat.

There were words and legacies. *Anung Un Rama*. The Crown of the Apocalypse. A name of destiny shunned and nearly lost so that it no longer held its greatest meaning. This secret somehow reminded him of his own forgotten name.

The power inside Jester rose up on its own accord, rearing in pain and exhilaration. Sweat burst upon his brow and he began to shudder, his pulse snapping hard in his neck, his heart hammering.

His hate was the hate of all men who twisted in faith and doubt, incapable of examining themselves too closely. He felt even closer to the demon now, understanding how they were both set on des-tined courses long before their births. They had become diverted and subjected to the will of others. To the endeavors of men and the testaments of Heaven and Hell. They had walked both paths, even if neither of them could fully remember who they'd once been.

Jester's arms were thrown open, his head pressed back as his mouth widened and the sparking black motes of arcane energy bled from his tongue, nostrils, ears, and eyes. His vertebrae popped and crackled as his spine straightened, and he started to rise into the air. His body hung like the form of Christ broken upon the cross.

Perhaps this was meant as tribute, perhaps only mockery. He began to laugh in his pain and fury—loving his own agony because it made him recall those who'd sinned against him, and reaffirmed his purpose in this world—until his mad laughter swept across the woodland and he slowly spun in midair above the demon's mysteries.

From the center of the churning secrets a great stone hand reached up and caught hold of Jester's ankle.

The dark preacher screamed in fear. His avenging rage struck down like a lightning bolt, scorching the ground, but the enormous fist would not release him. It began to draw him back to the earth. When he touched soil again, Jester dropped to his knees, exhausted, his clothes smoking. He was still grinning, but his eyes spun in terror. He knew more about what waited for him out in the swamp, and what would stand between him and his Sarah.

He sat on the dead child's blanket again and gentle fingers plied the worn threads at the shoulder of his frock coat.

The ghost of his murdered wife—*the wife he had murdered*—said, "Don't you let any harm come to my daughter."

She spoke in a voice that was somehow her own and yet had become much more since her death. She was filled with a strength and peace and light. The dead did not fret. The dead's concerns were only for love. She did not bear him any ill will, and she sometimes came to him with that repose and serenity which calmed his rage and the menacing intensity within him. She had power too.

"I won't."

"Sarah can't give you what you're hoping for. Neither can her baby."

He didn't shift to look at her. He hardly ever did. The face of her ghost was the face of the wife of the man he no longer was.

Yet it could still make him think of mortal, dreadful things. "You don't know what I'm hoping for."

"A'course I do. You still lookin' for family. The one you gave up for God."

"Doesn't that mean I deserve something?" he asked. His ruined voice was too awful for anyone living to note the whine in it, but the dead could tell. "Giving up all I had in worship to the Lord?"

"If you done it for payment you ain't done it from your heart or soul. You done it for the wrong reasons and blame Heaven for your own mistakes."

"I did it for love," Jester argued, "but I expected my wife to stay true to me."

"I made my mistakes too, but there ain't nothin' wrong in a woman needin' love. We gotta die alone but that don't mean we need to live alone."

"I do," he told her.

"You ain't alive."

She called him by his Christian name then, and the urge to look into her eyes was so great that he nearly turned to stare at her. But the selfish shadows twined around his body and held him tight, his face toward the endless glow of the bog where he'd find his daughter and grandchild.

His wife who was now one with Glory said, "You been dead near twenty years gone and too foolish to draw water from the pool of the hereafter."

"Leave me," he told her, and with nothing more than a hot breeze working across the forbidding earth, she did.

When the sun broke through the pines Jester rose from the slain child's blanket and entered the shack. Empty jugs of moonshine and bottles of wine littered the floor. He found the Ferris boys both still asleep.

Their dreams were laid bare to him. Duffy relived the moment of murdering their mother and father, which filled him with a fierce pride and some small vestiges of guilt. Over the years the corn liquor had worn the slight twinges of shame almost entirely away and allowed him to grin as he slept. Thinking of how his mama had screamed and their daddy had sneered that moment, as if they'd always been expecting it. Maybe they had. Duffy was only eleven, but big and strong for his age. Same with Deeter, who was ten.

They used freshly whittled ax handles they'd stolen from the dry goods store. Broke Daddy's arms first, then Mama's legs next, then took turns taking a swing at first one and then the other, counting off so they'd be all even steven. One-two, three-four, five-six, seven-eight. Got up to thirteen-fourteen before Farrell Ferris managed to drag himself from the shack and into the brush, where his sons followed him and watched him thrash among the thistles and catclaw briars. Deeter had gone back for the shotgun and used it to shoot Pa's big toe off. The flat harsh noise of the boys' laughter carried on into the deep sunset afterward, punctuated by a gentle but dramatic dripping, as if a spring rain had just risen over the woods.

The fervent mind of Deeter Ferris played on the rape of a nameless woman they'd caught four years ago after she'd turned off the highway hoping to buy some gator skins to make into a pair of boots for her husband. She was just driving slow through Enigma hoping to run into somebody who might be a gator killer. Damn near everyone was, but she just so happened to run across the Ferris boys, sitting out in front of Coover's garage while Coover finished reinforcing the suspension on their pickup in case they got into any more chases with the law through the hills while they were driving moon.

The boys took her back to their place and sold her a fine bull skin. No trouble on their mind that day, just enjoying the feel of her cash money in their hands and the gorgeous sight of her. Full-breasted, bleach-headed, the stink of the city on her like a musk. Then she went and fouled it up by talking about her husband, who sounded like a right fine boy until she got to the part about him being a correctional officer in Chadabunk School for Wayward Youths, which was where the Ferris brothers had been sent for nine years after the murder of their parents.

They reckoned if her husband was anything like the guards who'd brutalized them while they were there, then he was one self-righteous, billy club–wielding, ungodly perverted sumbitch who not only didn't deserve himself a fine pair of gator boots, but didn't justify having a right fine full-breasted, bleach-headed, musky wife neither.

She kept asking, What's the matter? as they tugged the gator skin out of her hands and took her purse away and Duffy got out her keys and drove her car away around back, and Deeter took her wrist and gently tugged her into the house. What's the matter? What's the matter? His muscles tightened and ached with remembering those words and how they'd soon contorted into screams.

Jester woke them with some reluctance, sharing in their joy and madness, and said, "It's time."

"Where we goin'?" Duffy asked.

"Into the swamp now. To find my Sarah."

"Pregnant girls in there, they likely gator bait already, bloated and ripening in some mud hole."

"No, they're alive, and we'll reach them tonight."

"And that big ole red fella?"

"If he stands in my way he'll suffer for it."

"We gonna need a skiff," Deeter said. "Ours got sunk the last big rain."

"You were drunk," Jester said, "and spilled moon on yourself while smoking a cigar you stole from a traveling soap salesman. You burned yourself and jumped in the water and the boat sank."

The Ferris boys watched him, the hinges of their jaws throbbing and the cold fear in their eyes, the way it should be.

A minute later Duffy scratched at his soft, golden stubble. "Plume Wallace got one down in the bottoms that he keep tied outside his shanty, over by Scutt's Landing. He's always on the look-out for crawfish."

"He ain't gonna like us takin' it. And he's got a shotgun."

Duffy opened an unpainted closet door and withdrew a twelve-gauge pump. "Well hell, looky there, so do we."

"Reckon I never liked that old boy much anyways."

"Let's go," Brother Jester said.

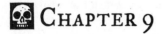 # CHAPTER 9

A low-lying mist shrouded the emerald hell, coiling upon the green darkness as the sky, the color of a bruise, grew brighter. Quickly the world amassed weight and substance, minute by minute growing in clarity, as if great hands were shaping each detail of life from scratch.

"Wake up, son," Lament said, and shook Hellboy's shoulder.

Hellboy was already awake, still curled beneath the blanket, staring at his stone fist. It was clenched tightly as if he'd been holding onto something. Even now he was a little worried to let go of whatever it was. He'd been dreaming deeply but he couldn't remember of what, and it took a while before he was able to open his hand and see that it was empty.

He sat up and noticed how the swamp not only looked much different in the light of day, but felt it as well. Fertile and vital but no longer imposing, there was a beauty here that he hadn't seen in the dark. Hummocks of scrub surrounded the tongue of land where they camped. Oleander and geranium blossoms added even more color so that the green jungle no longer overwhelmed.

The world around assailed him with so much noise that at first he almost hadn't been able to hear it. There were the sounds of crows, bullfrogs, polecats, skinks, egrets, squirrels, and ducks.

Hellboy was stiff and still sore from mixing it up with the gators. Gingerly he untied his makeshift bandages and was surprised to see his wounds looked clean and on their way to healing. He flexed his leg, did some deep knee-bends, and loosened up.

Checking the special cartridges on his belt, he held one up to the sun to make sure it wasn't damaged.

"What you got there?" Lament asked.

"A blood-soaked splinter taken from the wheel that broke the back of St. Catherine."

"Saints? Son, this is Southern Baptist Country. They ain't afraid of saints 'round here. They're afraid of Revenuers."

Hellboy persisted. "Stops djinn and Ambassadors of Mammon in their tracks, let me tell you. Guaranteed to slow down any member of the infernal order."

"Well, you'll surely hear a hoot of joy from me iffun we come 'cross any infernal order members thisaway."

Cool winds washed over the lake and whispered through the loblolly and catclaw briar. The old lady's ears told him which trees were which just by the sound of their leaves rippling in the breeze.

Pawing through his rucksack, Lament drew out provisions and started cooking breakfast. Hellboy spotted canisters of milk that should've curdled in this heat. He said, "Can I have a drink?"

Lament handed over the milk. Hellboy sipped it cautiously at first, and then drank deeply. It was cold and fresh. "Where'd you get this?"

"In town."

"Yesterday afternoon?"

"Tha's right."

"It should've gone bad by now."

"Enigma cows is fit."

Looked like Lament was making eggs, but much larger than those of a chicken. Hellboy watched him crack the shells and pour the yolks into a skillet he placed over the fire.

"Your stomach still distressing you any?" Lament asked.

Hellboy was surprised it wasn't. He was actually hungry. "No. I think I can eat."

"Glad to hear it. Pull up a patch of log here and come have breakfast. We got miles to cover and I fear the weather is gonna change. Now get you some bacon and corn griddle cakes."

"I like pancakes."

It took Lament ten minutes to make breakfast and serve it on tin plates. Until Hellboy took his first bite he hadn't realized how famished he was. The pancakes were sweeter and fluffier than he was used to, covered with a thick honey syrup. He ate quickly, enjoying himself. The bacon was thick and burned just right. The eggs were unlike anything he'd ever tasted before.

He knew he should let it slide, but he just had to ask. "What kind of eggs are these?"

"Turtle," Lament said.

Hellboy flipped his plate over into the dirt. "Gah!"

It got Lament chuckling softly again. Then snickering as he tried to hold in his laughter, but eventually it got away from him and he started guffawing, clutching his belly.

"It's not funny!" Hellboy shouted, though he found he was grinning himself. Strange to discover his mood had lifted in such an odd place as this. Still, a few minutes later, he realized he couldn't fully quit staring at his hand, trying to remember the dream.

"It wasn't a nightmare," Lament said, carrying the plates to the water's edge, where he washed them. "Not entirely. He come 'round visitin', Brother Jester did."

Hellboy didn't see any tracks in the dirt besides Lament's boots and his own hoof prints. "When? How?"

"He's got gifts. He's been blessed by the archangels. They haven't turned their backs on him just because he went crazy and became a killer. That's not their way. If they done that to everyone in the Bible who'd done lost their grace, there'd be no heroes at all. Sinning and redemption are at least as important as purity. They're fated to be with him no matter what evil he might do. They bear witness and whisper truths in his ear that no man should hear. Their shadows drop favors at his feet. They're just children lost without a heavenly father, searching for an earthly one. It's no wonder the prophets were all mad."

Angels. You just couldn't trust them. "Granny Lewt said you had a history with the walking darkness."

"Oh fer sure," Lament said, breaking camp, gathering up his provisions and repacking them. "I known him for a good long while now. Lot of rumors follow that old boy 'round."

"Granny said the same thing of you."

Lament nodded. "She's right on both counts."

"Who is he to you?"

"When I was a child, he was the man I wanted to grow up to be. Righteous, strong, full of God's word and a need to bring comfort and blessing to those who hurt. A man, I'm inclined to believe, much like yourself."

"And then he found out Bliss Nail was fooling around with his wife."

"That's right. And he went insane. Killed his own wife. Almost murdered Sarah in her crib."

"What stopped him?"

A gliding shadow moved out across the tree line and cut across the bright blue sky. Hellboy looked up and reached for his pistol, but it was only a white egret sailing through the air, its bill filled with squirming worms as it headed for its nest.

Lament was staring into space, lost in thought. His eyes cleared and his brow furrowed with the intensity of his memories.

"I did," he said. "I wasn't hardly eight years old, but I'd been singing gospel since I was old enough to speak. He had another name then. He come to town . . . this was up in the Appalachians, way back in the mountain woods . . . and he found me preachin'. He was famous by then, and I was but an orphan looked after by the whole town. Good God-lovin' folk, well, they wanted him to teach me in the ways of a travelin' pastor. So together we went off, and eventually come back to Enigma together. We preached in the swamps for a while 'fore he even set foot in his own house again. He loved the Word that much."

"It doesn't take much to derail a good man."

"That's the truth. He found his wife holding a newborn wasn't his own. Took no time at all for his heart to turn stone hateful. He run for the hatchet and I tried to stop him, but couldn't do much."

"You were only a kid," Hellboy said.

"And didn't fare so well. He brained me pretty good, ole Jester did. Then he went and murdered his wife, a kind and generous lady by all accounts. I prayed with the blood running out of me, and managed to stumble to where he was plannin' on stranglin' Sarah in her crib. And I prayed. A part of him that hadn't gone crazy and evil yet heard me. Anyway, he didn't get to kill her."

They finished packing up the goods together and Hellboy helped Lament load everything into the skiff. They both looked around one last time to make sure nothing had been left behind. Before they started off, Hellboy had one last thing he wanted to know.

"Are you the father of Sarah's baby?"

Lament glanced up, genuine shock and appall written into his features. "Considering we just met a few hours ago, and we haven't so much as shared a sip of moonshine yet, or even had a bite of gray squirrel or possum together, or passed a corncob pipe back and forth, and you done spit out the eggs I made, I reckon I don't see how it's any of your damn business, friend."

Hellboy shrugged. Jeez, these people were sensitive. "Okay. So where are we going?"

"Other side of the basin breaks up into more inlets that flush back into the marshes. The shanty town's in that direction."

"You've been there?"

"Not since I was a child. Me and Jester preached there once. But I recollect that's the way to go. The blackwater has a way of letting you know if you're aimin' right or wrong."

"How's that?"

"It either kills you or it don't."

Hellboy thought, That's what I get for asking. "Will we catch up to them today?"

"I reckon so. Sarah can move through the swamp with ease, but them other girls swole with chile have to be slowing her down some. Come on and help me with the skiff."

The keel of the boat had sunk a foot into the mud and they both had to grip an end and work it hard side to side before they could lift it to clear the rut. With a loud gurgle the drying muck gave way and the skiff came free.

"Hey," Hellboy said. "Something's been on my mind. Why'd you call me princely?" It had been a damn strange thing to hear.

Lament stared at Hellboy's head, or perhaps at the spot in the air just above his head, and his eyes gleamed with what could be a sad and distant knowledge he couldn't fully understand himself.

"Seems to me you're someone destined to wear a crown, tha's all."

# CHAPTER 10

They carried the skiff down the shore's incline back to the stale waters and stobpoled out of the mired shallows. They made their way through the curving narrows out into the lake. There, Lament boated the pole, slotted two oars into metal rings, and rowed them across the basin.

When they reached the other side Lament appeared to be unsure of which direction to go. Stunted dead sycamores lined the shore of another dark inlet, thick with hummock islands, matted with roots and silt. He rowed as long as he could, until the oars were stirring up deposits of sediment, then groaned and wiped his brow.

"Hell, boy!" Lament said.

"What?"

"What?"

"Oh, I thought you were calling me," Hellboy told him.

"I'm calling you a damn heavy heifer. Come spell me for a while."

It took Hellboy a second to figure out what Lament meant, but once he understood he moved up in the boat and took a turn at the oars. They started going around in circles. After a minute he realized he had to ease up on drawing too hard with his right hand, and finally got a good rhythm going.

Lament played the mouth-harp and then started to quietly sing. The song sounded vaguely religious and a little silly, but Hellboy enjoyed the sound of Lament's vibrant voice and even found himself humming along. When he realized what he was doing he frowned, shut the hell up, and rowed harder.

Broken tupelo spotted the area, the earth heavy with a peaty loam smell. They were entering a bog of maiden cane and wide draperies of hanging moss. Hellboy had a difficult time imagining people living out here. It had its own beauty but he just couldn't picture church folk coming out so far into the morass to hold revivals. Parents bringing their children this far for baptism and confession and gospel singing. All this green would have to drive a normal person out of his mind.

The oars struck root and the water churned with silt. The prow of the boat got trapped in log litter and mounds of slough as the small hummock islands thickened and their passage tightened.

"We have to row through all that?" Hellboy asked.

"Too shallow to stob," Lament told him. "I got to admit to my quandary though." He pointed at a trampled mud bank nearby. "That's gator ground for sure. They're everywhere. Watch that next log comin' up."

"I see it."

"It ain't no log. He's a big ole boy. Ding him and he'll chew the skiff to pieces. Skirt right."

"You sure the girls came this way?"

"No," Lament said, and left it at that.

Struggling with the oars, Hellboy put some more muscle into it and got the boat moving at a fair clip despite the thick grass and jetsam.

"Does she know you're coming to help her?" he asked.

"No, me and Sarah ain't talked in a couple months."

"Why not?"

Lament blinked a few times, like he couldn't believe the question. "I been adrift."

"But you somehow knew Jester was coming for her."

"I knew. I felt the shadows on me more than once, and I knew their intent."

Hellboy watched the hillbilly, thinking, Jesus, suspenders in this day and age. He felt oddly uneasy at the way Lament seemed to *put him* at ease. Humming along with that stupid mouth-harp, what was up with that? He knew he had to watch himself. Granny Lewt's spell might be working on him too well or the wet heat of the swamp was baking his brain, but something was having its effect.

Lament caught Hellboy's eye and said, "What?"

"I can't figure you out."

"Son, ain't we all got more than enough to do with figurin' on our ownselves? Without needin' to do it for other folks too?"

Sudden surface ripples broke against the side of the skiff. Drops of swamp water flew into Hellboy's face.

"We're coming to a bad spot," Lament said.

"A bad spot? What's that mean?"

"Can't you feel it?"

"No."

It would be nice to be able to feel a bad spot, Hellboy thought. Then he could step left or right instead of just plowing ahead the way he usually did. So no, he didn't feel a damn thing, and never did until some creep or another was trying to kill him.

But he could smell rain in the air, and he sensed how the swamp was beginning to hush and muse. "A storm's coming."

"It's already here," Lament told him.

A moment later the rain burst down upon them. One of those torrential downpours so powerful and immediate that they were both instantly as wet as if they'd fallen overboard. The wind rose and waves kicked up and washed over the bow. It was like they were lost at sea in a dinghy. Acres of watergrass waved about as if alive.

Hellboy realized they didn't have a pail and would very soon need to start bailing if they were going to stay afloat. Otherwise, they'd have to beach on one of the hummocks.

"I see a shack," Lament said. "Shore's closer than it looks."

"Is it the swamp village?"

"No, I don't think so. Just a loner out this far on the blackwater."

"We gonna knock and ask directions?"

"I reckon we will at that."

"But didn't you just say this was a bad spot?"

"I did," Lament said.

"Terrific."

It always came down to this. Heading into the place where you knew you shouldn't head.

Lament pointed to an area on the far bank of a small lagoon-like cove that eased away to a slimy shore covered with leaves and dead branches. The turbulent waters bubbled violently with rain. Lizards ran along the weeds as Hellboy brought the boat to a stop and he and Lament slogged to shore, dragging the skiff behind them.

The gray hanging mossbeard flapped and danced in the wind. Lightning skewered the skies. Lament parted the cypress streamers and climbed past the massive trunks. Strangler-fig vines as fat as garden hoses tangled around his legs and he nearly fell over. Thunder pounded. Hellboy reached down and clutched a mighty handful of the fibrous jungle vine in his right fist and tore away great lengths of it.

"You've got my gratitude," Lament said.

"Sure."

They continued on for another fifty yards on a slow incline until Hellboy saw the shack. It was a little larger than Granny Lewt's place but just as ramshackle and desolate.

Lament drew his wet curls out of his eyes and said, "It's Granny Dodd's place."

"She Granny Lewt's sister?"

"So I've always reckoned."

"Well, I'm telling you right now," Hellboy said, "I'm not eating anything, and if she tries to make me or if she's got a big brute of a son who aims to push me around, I'm going to knock somebody through the roof."

"I thank you for lettin' me know your intentions," Lament said. "But Granny Dodd's been dead a few years. Only her granddaughter Megan lives out here. 'Leastways I think so."

The storm kicked up another notch and the wind heaved the trees around, dead branches whirling and flying by, lost in the surrounding titi brush. Wind roared and wailed, alive with purpose. Rain pummeled like the angry hands of children. Lament turned to look at Hellboy. "There's evil will in the air." He pointed east. "Sun's still shinin' a mile or two off. Storm's breakin' right on top of us."

"Pretty standard where I go," Hellboy said. "Let's get inside."

They fought their way to the shack, both of them searching the heavy brush and mire for whatever they could see: pregnant girls, gators, walking shadows, who the hell knew what. Thunder shook the hanging willows and tattered beards of moss. Finally Lament got to the door of the shanty and pounded on it with the side of his fist.

A terrified woman's voice responded. "You go on and get away from my place now! I got me the two barrels of this here shotgun pointed right at you belly-high!"

"That you Megan Dodd? It's me, John Lament. You might remember me from some years back, when I used to sing in these parts as a child."

"You gotta be gone from here!"

Okay, Hellboy thought, so here it comes. The reason why this is such a bad spot.

"Why?" Lament asked.

"My man is gone. My husband . . . he . . . he gone away. He's been taken from me."

"Taken?" Lament asked. "By who? Who gone and done a thing like that, Megan Dodd?"

"You get on out of the blackwater now, you hear! Go on now!"

"Ain't no need to fear me or my friend here. Fact is, if you want a good belly laugh, feed him some turtle eggs."

"Hey!" Hellboy said. "Don't go starting any rumors."

"Ain't a rumor, it's a fact."

"What you want at my door?" Megan cried.

"I want to know if you've seen my Sarah and some other young ladies come through this way. They left Mrs. Hoopkins's home two days ago and I been trackin' them through the blackwater."

"No," Megan said, and that seemed to be the end of that.

"These are strange hours, and I need to find them."

"If they come this way they likely dead."

Lament froze in the rain and the wind hurtled and broke against his form at the door. He'd been bridling it well so far, but Hellboy could see how worried he was about Sarah and his unborn child. "Why do you say that? Who took your man, Megan?"

"Iffun you don't steer clear you gonna get took by Mama's girlies just as quick!"

"What are these girlies she's talking about?" Hellboy asked.

Lament shrugged. "I never heard tell of them before."

Hellboy could just see it. Roving bands of teenage girls, flaxen-haired and with their blouses knotted at their midriffs, wearing ragged jean shorts, glowering with cornflower blue eyes, running around in the swamp causing all sorts of damage. Men screaming and waving their arms in the air, ruffian girlies smacking them around. He turned up his ragged collar against the rain and scratched between his horns.

"Megan, let me in," Lament implored. "You gotta hold on now, and tell me what you're so afraid of. I felt it in the air, the cold and the cruel. What is it that's happened here since the last time I passed through."

"The Mama growed strong in the wooly patch," Megan whimpered. "I don't dare say she was never there before, 'cause Granny

Dodd, she knowed about it, kept the Mama at bay. But when Granny died, her spells grew weak and the swamp gone bad."

Lament tried the latch on the door and found it jammed. The resistance caught him off-guard and he spun in the silt and slime frothing beneath her shack, pitched sideways, and nearly dropped into it. Hellboy caught him and righted him, and their faces burned gold and then white in the flare of another eruption of lightning.

"Don't you come in," Megan Dodd whispered, her face pressed to the slats, the glint off her eyes and wet lips shining through the cracks in the planks.

"Why not?" Lament asked. "If you're afearin' this Mama and her girlies and your man gone missin', seems to me you'd be wantin' someone nearby to look out for you."

"It ain't me I'm a'fearin' for. You got to get on 'fore she learns you're here." The panic in her voice took on the tone of hysteria—words clipped with a little girl squeak, as if she were trying to crawl inside herself, or claw her way out.

Hellboy realized the whole wall of the shanty was groaning in protest beneath the heaving wind's onslaught, leaning horribly to one side. The years of rain and Spanish moss bleeding into the wood had rotted it until it was hardly more than tissue. He was afraid the next strong gust might blow the whole place down on the woman's head.

"Stand away," he told Lament, who refused to move aside.

"We can't push our ways in."

"Why not? I mean, it's wet out here. It's really wet out here."

"We can't go in unless we're invited."

"What are you, a vampire?"

"I abide by a code of manners."

"So do I," Hellboy said. "But it's really wet." He stuck out one finger against the knob and gave a little push. The door popped open and there was Megan Dodd, staring at them. She was holding the shotgun but the shells had broken open in her hands and the shot had spilled onto the floor. He could see they were so old they'd rotted in the humidity.

Long, dirty-blonde hair dangling mostly in her face, braided loosely on the left and clipped in tufts with broken pink barrettes on the right, Megan Dodd, granddaughter of another one of these witchy women had dark unforgiving eyes and a sorrowful presence. Who knew how many jars full of weirdo bits and pieces might be around here?

Middle-aged but with an air of inexperience to her, as if she'd been held back from the world and knew nothing beyond a hundred yards of the shanty. Both shoulder-straps had slid down her arms. The catclaw briar scars, sycamore scratches, and welts didn't mar her flesh in the least. Anywhere else she'd have appeared ridiculously child-like, but here it seemed natural, and more than that, perhaps even necessary. A peculiar and powerful musk like a bull gator's pervaded the shack.

She rushed across the wooden floor and hung back against the far wall. "Get away from me, O Lucifer, Son of the Morning!"

Lament moved, grabbed the shotgun out of her hand, and said, "He only looks like Lucifer. But he's a man of principle and his heart is righteous."

"You sure about that?"

"I'm certain. And look close—"

She peered at Hellboy for a moment and said, "Oh, those is Granny Lewt's eyes!"

Again with the eyes. He wondered when the eyes were going to wear off, or if when he got back to the rest of the world everybody would be commenting on his old lady eyes.

Megan came to some decision. "If she trusts him, I suppose I will too."

"What's going on here?" Lament asked. "Tell me what happened." An emerald wash of light ignited the side of her ashen

face as she passed a window. The caramel-colored freckles fleck-
ing her cheeks stood out as if etched, until she fairly glowed in
the interior of the shack. She pressed close to Lament. Slowly, she
brought her mouth to his ear. "You been gone a long while, John
Lament, but I remember your all-night sings in the church tents
when you was a child. You had the most beautiful voice. That still
the truth?"

"I don't know," he said. "I ain't sung much in recent times."

Hellboy almost mentioned the little song he'd sung in the rowboat on the way over, which in its own way had been beautiful and
captivating.

"Are you still a friend to the folks of Enigma?"

"You know I am."

"And the swamp folk too?"

"Yes. I'm your friend, Megan. Now you take a breath and calm
down some and tell me what's going on."

"You shoulda been gone, you shoulda gone, John." A bark of
frustration broke from her.

"Who are these girlies you keep mentionin'?"

Her face darkened with futility. "I can't rightly say. Granny
Dodd never let me go out too far in the lowland meadows. I
used to watch her throw her potions in the water and do those
rituals out 'neath the moon, and afterward she'd sleep for two
days straight so tired from makin' her spells'a protection. She done
warned me and my man Jorry, but he never did listen to her much.
Always used to say she wasn't right in her head. But Granny tole
us that Mama's girlies had a special need for men 'cause they could
be easily called away."

"Called away how?"

"I ain't got no idea, but called they were. After she died some of
the menfolk from 'round these parts went missin' and then my Jorry
got to thinkin' maybe somethin' was wrong after all. He never drifted
too far to get the gator meat. But three days ago Jorry went out into

the watergrass prairie and never come back. I spent all night and the next mornin' lookin' for him, but I failed. The girlies musta got him, and they gonna get you too iffun you stay here too long."

Dejection crowded Lament's face. He'd been hoping for more information about Sarah. He glanced at Hellboy and Hellboy told him, "Don't worry, we'll find her."

"I fear I done lost her trail already, and now the storm's gonna blow away any other sign. We'll stay until it passes and then be off."

"Back to Enigma," Megan said.

"No, I got to find her."

"She's likely dead as my Jorry."

"You done despair too easy, Megan Dodd, didn't your granny teach you no better than that? I gotta keep lookin' for my Sarah, and if I come across your Jorry, I'll send him back home quick-like."

Rain came on stronger, and the walls shimmied.

Hellboy warily took a sniff, and went into a fit gagging on the musk. When it finally ended, his throat was raw. "Christ, what is that?"

"I dunno," Megan said. "It started a week or so back, and gets stronger with the storms."

Taking up post at the window, Hellboy alternately stared out at the wet emerald hell and glanced down at his right hand, wondering what it was that he'd been holding onto in his nightmares. He kept getting the feeling that someone knew things about him that they shouldn't know, perhaps things he didn't even know himself or couldn't remember, and it pissed him off. He didn't like the idea of a rogue preacher out there spreading harm but still being blessed by Heaven. He realized then he very much wanted to meet this Brother Jester.

Lament and the girl talked about the swamp village. She'd never been there but she had an idea of where it was and which backwaters and inlets to take in order to get there. They had a different way of talking about water and mud and jungle than he'd ever heard. Sort of like how the Eskimos supposedly have a hundred different ways to describe ice and snow. Maybe it was true. He couldn't differentiate, but Lament seemed to understand the girl's ambiguous directions.

When the storm calmed some Hellboy looked over his shoulder and Lament was already saying goodbye to Megan Dodd.

She walked up to Hellboy and told him, "You jest watch out for Mama's girlies. You a man, like any other, least when it comes to that."

"Lady, give me a break, huh?"

Lament led him from the shack and the two slogged through the gurgling mud and mire back to the skiff.

"We'll find them," Hellboy said. "Take your own advice and don't despair."

"I'm doin' my best. But I fear."

The rain had cooled the swamp down, and the terrain had shifted dramatically with the deluge. The blackwater had risen enough that they didn't need to row the skiff anymore. The tangled roots and islands of matted branches were mostly underwater now, and as they pushed off they each reached for the stobpole.

"You done your part with the oars in the shallows," Lament said. "I'll take a turn."

"I don't like to just sit. I like to keep busy."

They each held the stobpole tightly. There was a moment when it could've gone either way. Hellboy could imagine the two of them slugging it out over which one got to shove the tiny boat around in the slimy inlets. They both needed action and wanted to let off a little steam. Hellboy just couldn't sit there staring at the glowing green any longer, trapped between boredom and serious tension.

Finally Lament released the stobpole. "Iffun you say, son. I'll guide us. Keep to the left here past the prairie grasses. I s'pect it's not the way Sarah and the girls came, but we'll hopefully meet up on the other side of this strait. The swamp village should be out thataway."

"You think we'll run into this Mama she was talking about?"

"Your guess is right as mine. Granny Dodd had her some real power to her, like her sisters. I reckon we'll find out what she was makin' or what she was fightin' soon enough."

Hellboy stobbed the skiff past the Spanish moss and along the inlets. Lament pointed and told him when to turn and how to avoid the jetsam. They worked well together like that for fifteen minutes. The skies cleared and the sun shone powerfully down. Lament signaled for Hellboy to stop.

"What's the matter?"

Drifting slowly in an eddy leading to a tussock of bull grass, low out on a sand bank, rested a crutch.

Poling more quickly as the skiff bumped up against the knolls and mounds of morass, Hellboy saw an overturned rowboat further along the bank.

Lament searched the waters. "Nothing else here I can spot. No bodies."

Hellboy nodded and saw a blur of black motion at the corner of his eye. He raised his chin and looked up.

"Hey!" Hellboy said.

"What is it?"

"I saw something."

"What?"

He pointed with his stone hand. "A girl."

Lament shielded his eyes from the sun and said, "Where? What girl?"

"A naked girl," Hellboy told him. "She was covered in flowers, way up in the trees, waving to me. Her eyes entirely black. As midnight."

# CHAPTER 11

Deeter Ferris stobpoled Plume Wallace's skiff through the morass with great efficiency and poise. His drunken, brutal father hadn't been good for too damn much, but the man had certainly taught his sons all there was to know about living on the bog.

"I still don't see why we had to bring this old boy along," Duffy said. "He startin' to stink somethin' awful. Passed a perfectly good sinkhole back aways where he'd'a been gone forever and not ruinin' our day. 'Stead we got a half a gallon'a blood sloshing in the bottom of the boat and evidence a'plenty if we run afoul of the sheriff or anybody else."

Brother Jester, seated in the back of the boat, held the corpse up beside him, his arm around Plume Wallace like he was hugging a drunken friend. The dead man's mouth was parted slightly, an inch of tongue jutting between the rotted stumps of teeth, with its ashen face still showing the frozen leer of a painful death on it, turned to Jester's ear.

Shadows twined around the corpse's lips and urged the secrets up from his undeparted soul. They slowly tore free like the deep roots of an old maple.

"Someone camped right there, at the edge of the basin last night," Deeter said.

"It was our enemies," Jester said. "We're growing nearer."

The long rumbling cry of a bull gator resounded like thunder across the weeds and hummocks, the gator's musk filling the air. Duffy drew his cutting blade, still crusted with Mrs. Hoopkins's blood, and cleaned it in the waters of the lake before replacing it in his sheathe. He saw the bull gator's rutted forehead skimming through the mire in the distance and watched his brother easily divert the skiff to avoid the beast. Duffy checked both the pump shotgun and the double-barrel ten-gauge they'd stolen from Plume Wallace's cold hand.

"'Sides that there weird-lookin' big red fella, who we aim to fight?"

Jester said, "An honest young man graced and blessed the way I was once graced and blessed."

Duffy waited for more and when no more was forthcoming asked, "That it? That all you gonna tell us?"

"That's all there is to tell the likes of you."

"Well, I figure a couple'a shell blasts in their gizzards are likely to stop them just fine no matter how weird or God blessed or graceful they be. What you say to that, Preacher?"

"I'm not a preacher anymore," Brother Jester told him, his ruined voice sounding even uglier as it snapped and echoed across the basin, imposing itself upon the natural sounds of the swamp. He turned his full attention to the corpse beside him.

Jester patted Plume Wallace's back—still wet with blood—running his hand back and forth and gripping a shoulder adamantly, the way a best friend offers condolences to someone lost in bereavement. Even after being shot twice by Deeter, it had taken Plume Wallace almost five minutes to die while crawling in the dirt behind his shack, drawing himself around and around in agonized circles.

He'd refused to plead or beg or beseech. He'd left the world cursing and reaching for Deeter's ankle. A man of pride and courage, Jester respected him deeply. Patting the body even harder, Jester felt a profound love for Plume Wallace.

All the dead had reasons to live, even if they didn't know those reasons while they were alive. Plume Wallace had a sister he hadn't seen in over thirteen years because of some fool argument they'd had over an old car radiator. Plume wanted to use the one in their daddy's junked Ford for his still, and she fought him on it because even a drop of radiator fluid would poison the moon and make him go blind. By God, but he knew how to flush a damn radiator he told her, what'd she think, that he was an eedjit? But she didn't want him to take the chance. She loved him too much and she worried. So he booted her in the ass and sent her packin' to go live with their lame Aunt Etta in Waynescross.

Only the recently dead understood real regret.

Now more than anything the spirit of Plume Wallace wished he could speak to his sister and beg forgiveness. She was right to have worried—he'd flushed that radiator plenty but when it was time to take the first sip of moon he gave it to his neighbor Earl Groell. Earl Groell was already mostly blind so it didn't matter much, but it didn't stop Plume Wallace from throwing the rest of the batch in the swamp and flushing that radiator again.

Now he sought to send his soul sixty-two miles northwest to the door of his Aunt Etta's home and pledge his love for his sister, even if she couldn't hear him. It was a need that consumed him, and the first step toward his shrugging free of his mortal self and finding peace at his entry into the beyond.

Jester's shadows held firmly to Plume Wallace's soul while it struggled to leave the rotting bag of flesh. The tortured expression on the dead face seemed to become even more despairing. "Not yet. Not yet. I have need of you, friend."

"What's he goin' on about?" Deeter whispered to his brother, and Duffy, the blood in the bottom of the boat rising halfway over his shoes, said, "Just you get us the hell out of these black waters, all right?"

Speaking quietly into Plume Wallace's cold ear, Jester told him, "Go on ahead of us. Visit with my true enemy. My shadows can see deeply in most things, but they cannot see him."

"I ain't your huntin' dog," the dead man told him. "Do your own damn villainous work, and let me alone. Sweet Jesus is waitin' on his throne to greet me comin' up the golden stairway. Ain't you done enough bad will on me?"

"You won't rest a wink in the afterlife until I release you, friend—"

"Ain't very friendly-like at'all . . ."

"And I won't do that until you aid me in my undertaking."

The dead were extremely sensitive. The ghost of Plume Wallace, already agitated because it hadn't found the peace of oblivion yet, grew angry and struggled harder to be free of its body. "That supposed to be funny? That what tickle your ribs, you skinny sumbitch? Mentionin' undertakin' to a murdered ole boy never done you no harm?"

"A poor choice of words," Jester admitted. "In my crusade to find my daughter and unborn grandchild in these dark waters I seem to have forgotten my manners."

Butting a log, the skiff jolted and shook, and the corpse flopped sideways away from Jester as if scrambling toward freedom. "I remember you now," said Plume Wallace's spirit. "I sat in on one of your gospel sings when I was no more than twelve, thirteen. You had a voice come straight from on high. You done good for folks, healed my mama's bunions, cured Daddy of a cyst in his eye. How'd you come to this?"

Smiling, his sorrow and madness entwined, Jester said, "I loved and I trusted."

Feathered shadows tugged at Plume Wallace's soul and Jester's hand ignited with his fury. He pressed his palm on the corpse's chest, shoving out the ghost but binding it to him. A thin silver strand no mortal could see connected them, and would until Jester decided to sever it and let Plume leave this world.

"Go on ahead and seek out my enemy. Find my daughter if you can, and return to me again with whatever you glean."

"I ain't got no choice, so I'll be back, and hope when I do I find you burnin' from your own malicious deeds."

"I already am," Jester said.

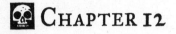# Chapter 12

Lament scanned the trees. "I don't see nothin'."

"I'm telling you, she was there," Hellboy said. "She waved to me."

"I ain't doubtin' you, son. If you say it's so, then I believe it."

"You don't sound like you believe it."

"Now don't you go gettin' all defensive on me."

"Christ, I'm not getting defensive!"

Tupelo, laurel, and titi shook in the breeze, and the swamp went silent except for distant murmurs that sounded like a man whispering sweet-talk to a loved one. Granny Lewt's ears didn't tell him it was any kind of a bird or rodent or reptile that only sounded like a man, so maybe it was Megan Dodd's husband Jorry or somebody else lost out there. He swung the skiff in that direction and came up against a thicket with dead hollowed-out trees jutting everywhere.

Lament froze and sucked air through his teeth.

"What is it?" Hellboy asked.

"Thought I felt somethin' for a second. Hold on."

Cocking an ear, Lament seemed to be listening intently to the wind, his curly hair wafting about his face. Hellboy saw that beneath the white streak was a large, old scar twisting across Lament's scalp. He thought about what that wound must've looked like on an eight-year-old boy and was shocked that Lament had managed to live through Jester's attack with a hatchet.

As if speaking quietly to someone nowhere in sight, Lament said into the breeze, "Plume Wallace, that you? This your silver thread?"

Then he made as if he heard some unheard voice. He frowned, nodded and grunted assent. "Uh yuh, yuh." Rubbed his beard stubble and listened a bit more. "I'm sorry to hear that, you was a pretty good ole boy, way I remember it. You done all that you could, don't fret none about that. You got my prayers to help ease your burden. No man should die crawlin' in the mud. And they stole your shotgun too? Sonsabitches."

Hellboy said, "Hey, I'm right here, why don't you tell me what's going on?"

Lament held a hand up and gestured for him to wait. After another minute the hillbilly's face reddened and he tightened his fists. "Goddamn them Ferris brothers. They such handsome boys they got near everybody beguiled. I shoulda killed them when I had the chance. You tell Mrs. Hoopkins she gonna rest easy, I'll see to her girls. Bliss Nail owes us all a little somethin' for settin' us on this damn course, he got the money to keep her home and peanut farm runnin'. Maybe he can get his own six daughters out helpin' folks, leadin' their lives again. I'll make sure he finds the good Samaritan in himself and becomes a fine and charitable person, you got my word."

He faced Hellboy and said, "Jester's onto us. Got hisself a couple of bad ole boys, too, name'a the Ferris brothers. Killers born and bred, though they're golden-haired and beautiful to gaze on. They cut down Mrs. Hoopkins a short time after you left last night."

"Damn it."

"And this morning they stole the skiff from a fella name'a Plume Wallace. Worse than that, Jester's put his soul in service to learn what he can about us. He ain't seen Sarah or the girl you spotted in the trees a'drape in flowers, but the dead are sensitive and he knows we comin' up to a bad area of the blackwater."

"Seems that's all we've been doing. Is there a good area in this swamp? I don't like being chased. I'm the one who does the chasing."

But Lament turned away to dialogue with the ghost again. Hellboy checked the cypress and the sycamore and pine trees once more. A naked girl with flowers wreathed around her body wouldn't have been nearly as unsettling if she hadn't been forty feet in the air and had eyes black and empty as a shark's.

"Let me see if there's anything I can do," Lament said to the dead.

With the poise and fluidity of performing a well-practiced ritual, Lament moved his hands into the proper positioning for casting a spell. Interlaced, with the tips of index fingers together in a this-is-the-steeple fashion, his thumbs pointed over his heart. Hellboy could feel the straining effort of Lament's will in his perfectly conducted actions.

Bursts of blue and black sparks crackled in his hands. The hillbilly drew hexagons in the air, followed by a seal of Solomon, pentacles, representations of the Sephiroth and Sephirah angels, and Kabbalistic symbols.

Hellboy recognized the Rite of Release, which set free bewildered souls that still thought they were alive. But he'd studied for decades reading ancient grimoires and tomes in the finest paranormal libraries of the world. Where could an Appalachian-wandering, mouth-harp-plucking, former-child evangelist, backwoods drifter learn all this?

Visibly weakened and shaken, Lament wavered and sat heavily in the skiff. "I'm sorry, Plume Wallace. His whipcord is too tight upon your soul. He's a long row of bad, but liar ain't among his evils. Iffun he said he'd let you go, he will. I promise to tend your grave least once a year, no man deserves less than that."

The breeze rose and shook leaves down on them, and then it fell away and the swamp was silent and still again. For an instant Hellboy thought he saw a reflection of silver in Lament's eyes like a trail of mercury floating by, and then it was gone.

He didn't mind following his instincts and going along blindly with a situation when there was no other way to approach it. But he didn't like being in the dark when someone else knew a hell of a lot more about things than he did.

"I've had it with you," he said. "Who taught you that Rite of Release and those other magic practices? Where did you learn them?"

"I ain't never learned no such thing," Lament told him. He pulled the small jug of moonshine from his rucksack and took a sip, screwing his face up at the taste. "They learned me."

"That doesn't make any sense."

"Mayhap not, but it's still the truth."

Hellboy took up the pole and pointed it at Lament's chest. "I want some answers from you, pal."

"If I had 'em to share, then share 'em I would."

"That sounds pretty, but I'm not buying it. I've seen a lot of strange things in my time, but you're starting to make me really antsy."

"Well, boy, I done told you that none of this is your burden, and iffun you wanted out, I'd point you the way any time you like." Lament replaced the jug and took hold of the stobpole with one hand, pointed into the jungle with the other. "That's how you leave, 'cept you'll have to swim and crawl and walk to get out, 'cause I still have need of this boat. But you'll make it, I'm sure of that. You ready to be on your way?"

"I'll see this thing through to the end," Hellboy said.

"Well, you follow your heart as you see fit, son."

Hellboy drew in a deep breath, ready to launch into a lecture about the times he'd been betrayed by those he thought were his friends. He jutted his chin and took a step forward when he saw several beautiful naked women wearing flowers draped about their bodies and in their hair, coyly flitting about in the brush.

"Oh crap."

"That about says it." Lament snatched the pole out of Hellboy's hand and started stobbing the skiff along fiercely. "Those must be Mama's girlies, whoever or whatever they be. We need to get on away from here."

"Well, yeah," Hellboy replied, "sure, but—wow, they're pretty—"

And that's when the boat got caught on the edge of a tussock of briar and bull grass, where a naked old guy lay in the shallow muddy water, giggling insanely to himself.

Okay, Hellboy thought, so this place had weird people just everywhere you looked. You couldn't walk on a road or climb into a boat or get lost in a swamp without tripping over them. Given a choice, he'd rather be glancing around at the nudie cutie-pie girlies than looking at this guy's wrinkled pale patootie.

Hellboy leaned over but couldn't quite reach the geezer. "Ease us in a little closer. You know who he is?"

Lament shook his head. "No, never met him, 'leastways not that I recall."

The deranged coot crawled through the slough, dragging himself by his arms over the matted roots and silt teeming with white egrets and other life. His legs were thin and twisted, and he was apparently crippled. That would explain the crutch they found. His laughter came from deep in his bony chest. From all about in the brush, girlish titters seemed to echo it.

Lament worked them around the tussock toward the old man, who was trying to scrabble across the bank of branches on his useless legs.

"Ma girlie," he said. "Smellin' so pretty and so fine. She was here, jest for me, singin' the way I like. Leave me alone, I say! Go way now, you go on away!"

"Come on, old-timer," Hellboy said, lifting the guy into the skiff, "let's get you out of the water." The geezer weighed hardly anything. He was undernourished, dehydrated, and exhausted, as if he'd been lying out there doing nothing but smiling obscenely for days. "What's your name?"

"Ain't got one!"

"You don't have a name?"

"Not no more. Please, I never done you no harm. Put me back. Put me back!"

"We're going to take you home."

"No, I say, no!" the coot cried. His beard was tangled with thorns and he was covered in the jetsam of the bayou. His skin was raw from sunburn and insect bites. Hellboy wrapped him in a blanket and tried to get some of the corn griddle cakes down his throat, but the old man refused to eat.

Turning away, Hellboy caught a powerful musky perfume on the air.

"Smell that?" he asked.

Lament nodded. "Same odor that was in Megan Dodd's shack."

"Cain't go back no more," the old man whimpered. "Hep me get on. I needs to get on with my answering."

Something bumped against the bottom of the boat, and Hellboy almost lost his footing. Lament tried poling free and said, "We're stuck on water vine."

Staring into the marsh prairies, Hellboy knew a fight was coming with whatever was down there. The waters were thick with silt, snaking roots, and rotting clumps of plant matter. Although the cypress reached astounding heights here, sunlight broke through and lit the black waters, the green mire glowing, alive and hungry and eternally patient. He tightened his hands into fists waiting to slug something.

Then he saw it. A hand *waving from beneath the slime*, as if gesturing for him to follow. Red fingernails wrapped with a thin, veil-like film.

"There's somebody down there," he said.

"No one we want to cotton with. You're much stronger than me, come pole us out of this patch."

"My girlie!" the geezer cried.

A mass of ebony fibrous hair now wove about in the waters, and the giggling of the girls continued to waft among the trees.

Calling to the skiff and calling to one another. The perfume grew
stronger. Hellboy turned and spotted the flash of limbs among the
tupelo. An arm, a breast, a well-muscled leg here and there. A smile,
a glimpse of dimpled thigh.

Eyes without pupils, staring: black, lethal, empty.

"Take the stobpole!" Lament shouted.

Hellboy grabbed it and shoved the skiff off the tussock with a
groan of snapping branches. He watched as the hands beneath the
water still came reaching for them. Those ladies were holding the
boat in place. Laurels and flower petals shook from the trees and
heaved from the swamp bottom.

Below, the girlies stared up at him. Beckoning, hauntingly
beautiful and lush as the jungle itself. As he stobbed he brushed
their bodies, and could hear vines tightening in the water, like a
snare netting them. "We're getting tied up."

Lament looked left and right, trying to find a way out of the trap.
"Old man," he said, "this call a'yours. What are you answering?"

"You hear it, don't ya? If not, you will. You gonna hear and see
and smell and feel the girlies in the grasses."

"Who are they? What are they now?"

"All I love and ever wanted to love and care for," the coot
cried, laughing, his crooked legs bouncing wildly as the skiff
jounced.

"You're already a week or so starved. Another few days and
you'll be dead."

"Don't matter none to me! Let me go on with the rest!"

Lament's face hardened. "The rest? Where are they?"

"We all happy, damn you. Why'n't you just let us be?"

The blackwater churned, faces appearing in the mire around
the keel. The women rose and dove, almost invisible as they swam
and played. Hellboy stobbed harder and the tendrils below tightened around the pole and tried to yank him in.

"This is getting ridiculous," he said.

"Gator on the left," Lament said. "He ain't lookin' edgy or angry at'all. Guess he's used to these curious inlets."

The scut-backed bull came out of the swirling from the morass, and hands broke the surface of the water, fingers pointing. With a wild cry of desire, the crippled old man threw himself overboard and went under, rising instantly to let out a single scream—perhaps joy or maybe terror now—and Hellboy was too slow getting a hand out to him.

The geezer flapped his spindly arms trying to stay afloat, glaring and shouting in surrender. "My girl ... she's here ... !"

"Old fool, swim back to us!" Lament called. "You got a bull sidling up behind you!"

" ... She's here ... ! My girl ..."

The gator accelerated and snapped its jaws firmly on both the coot's feet. He didn't appear to feel anything and hardly made a face as his blood bubbled and seethed around him. He continued grinning, trying to move to the beautiful forms ahead.

The gator took him below, rolling and thrashing. Vines snapped taut and hummed like the strings of a guitar. More women broke from the brush, boughs and tree limbs cracking as they moved into sight and instantly out again.

"Jesus Christ," Hellboy said. "What is it with these broads?"

"I just don't know. Maybe Granny Dodd did somethin' to them, or mayhap she was fightin' them, tryin' to control them."

Blood thickened in the water and the girls swam about in the crimson froth.

"Can you get us free, son?"

"This whole area is choked with weeds, grass, and vines ... and people ..." He had to be careful not to snap the pole. He leaned over the bow and reached down, grabbed a handful of the water vines and tore them loose. The skiff loosened and swung aside. Lament took hold of the stobpole and pushed off. They skimmed more roots and drifted another dozen yards.

Then Hellboy saw them, laid out in vague rows like rice paddies.

They lay in the mud shallows, the swamp men who'd answered this call and followed the scent.

Some had drowned and others had been bled while entwined with their girlies. Like the geezer, those men died with smiles, their eyes rolled back in their heads, tangled in the mire. Crowding into thickets and acres of morass. Those still alive didn't notice the skiff entering their patch of bayou grassland.

The women looked up from their prey, leering, their red nails bright in the sun. Hair floated like tasseled black dresses, eddying in the green fen. Innocent faces too empty of sin to be human glanced over at them from every direction now. They were all the same woman, with identical faces and bodies.

"Lord a'mighty . . . wait . . . the smell, it's . . . " Lament said in a daze.

He reached for his shirt pocket but never made it. His eyes rolled up in his head and his lips twisted into a crazed smile. Moaning, he collapsed and fell over backward into the water.

Hellboy moved but it felt like he was buried in mud. He watched the swamp men in the muck shuddering and mewling, reaching for their girlies. He looked for Lament but couldn't finish turning his head to the side.

The heavy stench became overwhelming and sickening, enrapturing and engulfing his thoughts. Swooning, he realized too late what was happening.

The musk, it was some kind of narcotic—

This was a nest.

A farm.

Where the girlies fed on men.

Two gorgeous women swam up and climbed from the shallows, white and pink flower petals falling and filling the boat. They each took hold of one of Hellboy's arms and gently tugged. He closed his eyes and dropped into the emerald hell.

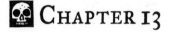# CHAPTER 13

Cries of children drew him awake.

Shadows passed over and through him, his memories stirred and his green dreams tinged with prophecy, forcing him back to the world. Children. Inhuman, horrific in nature. Calling to God and those who aid God's will.

A woman's tongue probed his neck. Hellboy threw his head back and made an effort to open his eyes. Everything stayed dark. Perhaps it was night, or maybe he'd been blinded. This kind of blackness, it somehow felt eternal. Then he realized he still hadn't opened his eyes and he tried again.

Sunlight filtered through the soaked cypress. Girlies moved jerkily before him, in a slithery, sexual fashion. Arms and legs moving in perfect concert with the dead and dying men coiled in the waters. So incredibly beautiful, these women. Plump and rounded, with thin calves but heavy wide hips, breasts heaving in the cutting golden rays. Their nails weren't painted but dripped blood and tissue torn in thick strips from men's backs.

"I bet this is bad," he muttered.

His voice sounded strange to him. Weak, doped up. He looked around and found that he was kneeling in the water with the bull grass surrounding him, tendrils tangled around his legs, arms, and throat. He made a feeble attempt at breaking free and the tendrils tightened, choking him until he nearly passed out again.

Women—*dozens of the same woman*—wove all about him, lissomely dancing and wafting, biting him and drawing blood. There wasn't much pain but it did sting, and he held onto the small aches and tried to concentrate and center himself.

He said, "Hey, hey . . . lay off."

They tittered, and it wasn't a human sound. More like wind blowing through boles in a tree, the scratchy noise of leaves brushing together.

"I don't suppose . . . you ladies . . . can talk . . ."

Several turned to face him and he got his first good look at those eyes—those awful catfish eyes. Jesus Christ, back to the catfish, always with the catfish. He didn't like them any better now than he had on his dinner plate. The girlies tickled him under the chin and kept making small wounds to sip from. They rubbed the flowers, wreathing them over his nose. They opened their mouths and he saw shards of yellowed, brown, and black teeth in there— mercury and gold fillings, bent bridge work.

One of the women pressed the side of her face to his stone hand, trying to bite into it. He pinched his fingers closed and grabbed her upper lip. She pulled away with a soft ripping sound and half of her face lifted easily and flapped free. The rest hung from a fractured skull that had been cracked decades ago.

Their flesh wasn't flesh at all, but a plant-life designed to appear as skin, grown over the skeletons of men who'd died out here in the swamps maybe a hundred years ago. The black hair was some kind of stringy, grass-like fiber.

Hellboy shrugged at the vines again, tightening the muscles in his throat to hopefully keep from strangling himself. They pulled taut as the women cavorted, lifting and leaping through the air, flying. At last he saw that the tendrils were actually *attached* to the girlies.

The vines moved the women about like marionettes. The girlies, they weren't separate creatures. They were all part of *the same being* . . .

A plant posing as dozens of beautiful human women, to bait and entrap men.

So they were all Mama—another living part of the bog, a single life-form that made use of the rotted dead on hand. Surviving and reproducing on living blood, always hungry and feeding on others.

One woman touched his mouth and crammed a finger down on his tongue. Then she did the same to herself, moving her lips to mimic speech as the air was driven through the . . . the what? . . . stalk? . . . stem of a blooming flower? The bellowed air produced a harsh whistling noise almost like laughter.

The noise was weird but lulling. Flower petals kept falling from above. Hellboy strained against the tendrils, pulling harder and harder, grunting and hauling forward. The women flinched and heaved around him, hoisted from the water. He kept tugging even though he couldn't breathe, a small surge of adrenaline limping through his veins.

There were a lot of unacceptable ways to die, but going out as plant food had to be damn near the top of the list.

His lungs began to burn and so did his mind, red and black flares rising at the edges of his vision. He opened his mouth to cry out but he didn't have enough air. Still he continued straining, pushing himself, the scream rising inside along with the fire until finally there was a deafening whip-crack blast, followed by another and another. Like tree bark being sheared by lightning strikes. The vines snapped away and the pressure eased.

It took him a while to catch his breath. Half a dozen of the girlies appeared to be dead in the water around him, floating face down and carried into the bull grass by the rippling waves his struggles had caused.

He reached for his gun but his holster was empty. He searched the rows of dying men until he spotted Lament, who was also weakly grappling with a girlie, his mouth twisted into a melancholy smile. She had scraped a particularly deep gouge along his ribs, and her palms and chin were covered with his blood.

Hellboy shrugged forward and moved to them. He stretched his arm down into the bog, got his stone hand on the creature's ankle, and pulled hard. The suck of sediment and slime resisted for a moment, and then with a great bubbling sputter she came loose. Free, her legs whipped against Hellboy with extraordinary force and he was nearly batted aside. One foot caught him solidly in the jaw as she slithered loose.

Lament groaned and reached into the air where she dangled with one long fleshy tendril snaking back down into the slough, connected to the center of her back. She smiled, still crooning, suspended in midair as the vine lifted higher and vaulted her across the area. Her left leg had snapped at the knee, bent backward at an awful angle. On display was all the long-dead bone, root, tubers, and moss that comprised her.

The woman lifted again and darted toward Hellboy, the tendril swinging her into flight. He caught her face in his right hand and crushed her head, the ancient skull beneath bursting into fragments.

Mama finally realized the threat.

A reflection caught his eye. He looked and it was gone. He set off for the spot in the grass where he'd seen it.

Another woman fell atop him and clung to Hellboy's back. She dug her fingernails in, and he realized they were actually thistles and barbs for easily rending flesh. She dug them in deeply, and he let out a cry, trying to tear her free. After whirling about, he managed to get a hand on her wrist and tug her arm loose from the shoulder.

She writhed in the cypress overhead, beckoning with her remaining fingers, and moved to him again.

Hellboy thought, What I wouldn't give for some industrial strength weed-killer.

There was still a loving expression on that lovely face, the catfish eyes empty of any humanity. He hit it again, and again, and once more until the woman's body tore free from the tendril. She dropped motionless beside one of the dying men laid out in his aisle. The guy lethargically propped himself in the mud and started wailing as his girlie sank into the slime.

The tittering grew louder until it was more like a scream in the underbrush. The cypress shook and rattled, more women gliding in and rising from the waters, joining the fray. He couldn't keep this up much longer the way he was feeling. His thoughts were still sluggish, his head stuffed with cotton and razors.

Hellboy called, "Lament! John Lament! Get your hillbilly butt up, I need some help here! All you other guys, if you want to live then come on, fight! Fight it!"

He slogged ahead and spotted the flash of metal again, near his feet. He stormed forward and found his pistol half-buried in weeds, caked with mud and slough. He quickly tried to clean it on his coat but nothing was helping much.

"Son of a—"

Another marionette dropped on him and he drew back his fist to pummel it, but its jaws cracked wide and its neck distended like a snake's to fit his stone hand down its throat.

He tried to pull free but the girlie tightened her hold and began gnawing her way up his arm.

Terrific.

He was already trying to figure out what he was going to put in his report and what he'd leave out. Some of this stuff was pretty embarrassing.

The girlie began moaning with hideously false noises. He pressed the gun to her forehead and saw the barrel ease into the flesh-like fibrous growth. He pulled the trigger and the barrel exploded.

Agony lanced through his left hand and he cried out. The force threw him backward into the shallows and the human skull in the girlie's head came along with him in a splash of bayou silt.

How do you kill a weed? You have to tear it out by the root.

All the girlies started rushing forward in unison, trying to drink the blood from his wounded hand. Lament raised his head and began to fight with the creatures too, like some kind of celebrity being mobbed by fans, sinking beneath their numbers. They dragged him away deeper into the ooze.

 CHAPTER 14

After wetting a bandana and wrapping it around his neck, Duffy Ferris pointed to the inlet at the base of the dark lake and said, "I see they broke camp over that'a'way this mornin'. There's still a faint trail of smoke risin' from the last of their embers."

"I see it too," Deeter said. "That's gator ground."

"Crossed over to the other side and goin' deeper into the morass. Notice where they tore up the twigs passin' through? All the mud they raked up and log litter they broke past? We comin' up to the marsh prairies. We're only two, three hours behind 'em."

"I spot two cold camps," Deeter said, shielding his eyes from the sun. "One a bit aways from the other. Them teenage girls come through this way too, mayhap the night before. None'a them are gator bait yet."

"Which ain't to say there ain't still a chance for it."

"No, which ain't to say that at all. Gotta admire them girls' pluck though. All of 'em with child. Ain't a one of 'em that's what you might call weak-willed."

Duffy grabbed the pole and began stobbing again, his muscles corded and the thick veins twisting along his arms. "You think Dorrie Mae Wilkes is among 'em?"

Deeter furrowed his brow. "Which one's that?"

"Pretty young thing, blonde hair halfway down her back, fine shapely figure on her. She won Miss Peach Pit over in Waynescross last summer, rode up front on the float during the Peach Pit Parade. You don't recall?"

"Wilkes's got four girls, so I'm havin' some trouble decipherin' which particular one she might be."

"Don't matter none." With nostrils flaring, Duffy sniffed the air. "You smell it?"

"Can't smell me nothin' but that ole boy gettin' riper in the back of the damn boat."

"Corn griddle cakes. And fried turtle eggs. No breeze here to carry the aroma off."

"Yeah?" Deeter put a hand on his belly as it emitted an audible growl. "Them boys are livin' the honeyed life out here, for certain. Wish we could stop for some food. It's gettin' on lunchtime."

Duffy whispered, "That Jester don't eat but what he finds flattened dead on a broken white line, so I guess he expects the same of us. How I do wish we never run into that hell preacher."

"No more so than me," Deeter said. "Bless my ears, I hear him still conversin' with that deceased codger."

"Naw, he done quit that a while back. Guess ole Plume Wallace wasn't reciprocatin' enough. Now preacher's just prayin', except they ain't like no prayers I done heard any man mutter before."

The Ferris boys turned together to check on Brother Jester, who sat in the stern of the skiff with the corpse, doing little besides mumbling and staring. The flies were so heavy back there that a dark cloud hovered and wreathed about Jester, who didn't seem to notice.

They both thought, He gonna eat that old boy?

Jester's shadows let him know this. It almost made him smile.

He'd eaten much worse things than human flesh. He'd supped on his own venom, he'd swallowed the tenets of God's law. He'd drank from puddles of rain provided by the great seraphim. Warm waters which tasted of the great flood and Noah's destroyed earth. Tasting God's wrath and the near-end of humanity in stagnant pools by a roadside—now that weighed on a man's heart. Or it would've, if Brother Jester had still been a man.

The silver whipcord thread chimed beside him and he felt the impeding return of Plume Wallace's ghost rushing toward the skiff.

After a moment the spirit appeared and Jester asked, "How went your mission?"

"Weren't no damn mission," the bound ghost said, "just a wrong-hearted errand you sent me on. Like we dead got nothing better to do all the long day but attend your beck and call. My first wife Ettie, now she was a lot like you, son. Would get it into her head at all crazy hours of the night that she needed herself some Epsom salts for her foot bath, like I'm'a gonna go be able to find her salts at three in the morning just 'cause she got bad corns. Yeah, you and Ettie got a lot in common—"

"I want an answer," Jester said. There were just as many flies crawling across his forehead as there were on Plume Wallace's ashen brow. "What did you see?"

"You already know what I saw, you sent me to go see it."

"Stop being contrary."

"The morning a man's murdered for his boat and his poor wracked body brought along on a snipe chase is a day meant for bein' cantankerous, I say. But all right, all right, I'll tell you what you crave. I seen John Lament, growed up. Side by side with a big red fella lookin' a little dinged up hisself. They're up yonder, across the basin in a bad patch of land, where the wind is colder and the jungle got itself teeth." The ghost grinned with its ethereal lips. "John Lament. All these years gone and still you a'fear him, the one who was just a boy at your bent knee, learning the ways of God by your very own tutelage."

"I know his past as I know my own. I didn't ask you about that."

"And I'd say you still need to hear about it anyways, 'lest you be forgettin'. You ain't minded your Bible, preacher. You reapin' what you done sown."

Brother Jester's hand began to burn. It ignited buzzing flies and soon the air was filled with their blazing flights until they all disintegrated. Jester plucked at the silver cord connecting spirit to corpse. It vibrated and hummed like a choir of ill children, and Plume Wallace winced and let out a sob. "Lord God, no, don't do that. It—it pains me so—"

"God not only can't help you, child of man, but He won't. He chooses not to, as is His way. I control your afterlife. I can leave you in oblivion forever if I choose. Such is my power, instilled in me by His very angels." Jester pulled at the thread and drew the ghost to him until they were nose to nose. "I serve God's purpose. He decrees this to be your fate, not me."

"No, it ain't possible, a foul critter like you. It just can't be . . ."

"It is," Brother Jester told him, and a hint of sadness entered his voice. "But you'll meet the Lord this day and then you can argue His folly to His great beatific face if you so choose. But first you're obligated to me. Now tell me what I wish to know."

"I done told you already what I seen."

They passed close to the shore as Duffy Ferris stobbed them toward the inlet to the dark lake, palmetto leaves and fronds pressing in on the skiff. Some loblolly berries fell and bounced off the face of Plume Wallace's corpse and rolled across his blue lips. The phantom jutted his tongue as if trying to taste the sweet flavor one last time. He reached to touch his own chin but he couldn't put a hand to that flesh anymore.

"You're a ghost now, not bound to body or the five senses. Tell me what you know beyond your being. Stop your chattering and say what you experienced and brought back with you."

"But I . . . wait, there was . . . they were in a bad spot, rife with murder." Surprised by his own phantom knowledge, Plume Wallace began to speak of what he hadn't witnessed but still somehow perceived. His gaze took on that same faraway, understanding clarity that Jester's wife's eyes had. His voice lost some of its expression. "That's right, they're in a bad place of pain. There were many other who were dying or already gone, all of 'em with smiles on their faces."

"Yes?"

"They been brought to a patch of swamp used as a farm . . . a blood farm. They went about writhing, in the graceful arms of the swamp itself." The ghost made as if to wipe sweat from its brow. "I don't like this sight. I ain't cut out to be deceased!"

"As much as any of us, Plume Wallace!"

"Well, they heard as much about the men gone missing from Granny Dodd's granddaughter, Megan. Granny Dodd, she's gone now too, poor woman, and her witchy ways are weakening. The chains she forged to hold back evil have broken. And I presume she's handling her state of interment better than me. Better than I will, once I get interred, is my meaning."

"What of the demon, what do you prophecy of him?"

"Ain't no demon, just a big ole red fella tryin' to help out some folks in trouble. He's powerful, tinged by great fate. He's got an admirable heart. You recognize that already. He's got a good many blessings on him. He's righteous. So's Lament. He's got grace, that boy, an old and wise soul."

"And my daughter?"

"I ain't seen nor felt her passin' by, neither livin' nor otherwise. Can't tell you nothin' more."

Brother Jester nodded, "Then go on now, Plume Wallace." He held the silver thread up to his mouth and snapped it apart with his teeth. "I release you from this earthbound custody. Go on up the jeweled stairway to Jesus, if you think you can find it."

He tossed the cord into the wind, but the ghost of Plume Wallace continued to sit in the skiff another moment. He said, "God got you in His sights, son. He'll be comin' for you soon enough, devilspawn."

And then was gone.

But his words struck Jester as wonderfully amusing. Absurd even, considering his own damnation and who he now followed. Devilspawn. He snickered as he shoved at the corpse beside him and threw it into the lake, watching it roll over behind them.

On the far shore two bull gators crawled down a hillock of mud and began to swim toward the body. Jester couldn't control himself and continued laughing until he was whooping.

The Ferris boys moved closer together in the bow of the skiff, staring at the madman. Brother Jester tossed his head back and howled, and the black clouds ushered in across a sky of pain.

 CHAPTER 15

Sometimes you just had to prove to some giant monstrosity or another that survival of the fittest didn't have anything to do with size.

For some reason they all got it into their enormous heads or manifold forebrains or multifarious cranial casings that they could just mow over folks because they were bigger or faster or a little nastier than most everybody else.

That's why, when you got right down to it, Hellboy's function was knocking over the biggest creeps on the block and showing them there was something even worse around.

He reached underwater and filled his stone hand with several of the mother vines, secured his grip, and tugged hard, holding the women back from Lament.

This whole trip was starting to get on his nerves. Hellboy muttered, "That's enough of this crap," and with a powerful wrenching motion that made him bite into his tongue, he jerked until the tendrils connected to a half-dozen women started to rip loose.

Their limbs flailed, those luscious mouths opened as if to scream, but all they emitted was that same noise of the wind through the woods. He grimaced and pulled harder. Those catfish eyes gazed at him, incapable of sadness or any kind of honest pleading for mercy. That was something to be thankful for. He swallowed the taste of blood and roared, and with one powerful final twisting yank he separated the bodies from the vines and the rest of Mama.

The no longer animate husks fell into the muck and immediately began to sink. Lament came sputtering up from the mire.

Suddenly the remaining girlies hovering over the dying men were snapped back through the brush. They flew high into the trees and thickets and vanished.

A hush fell over the area broken only by the soft, lonely whimpers of the few emaciated men who hadn't yet perished. Soon even that stopped. Hellboy stood ready, checked behind himself, and watched the water.

Yeah, sure, like he was going to believe it was all over and drop his guard now.

He made his way to Lament, who floundered in the shallows choking and spitting out weeds and blooms. Hellboy got his arms around him, pulled him to his feet, and held him securely while Lament vomited.

It took him a while to clear his guts. When Lament was through he pressed himself to Hellboy's chest and stood there wide-eyed and shuddering.

"You all right?" Hellboy asked.

Okay, so it was a stupid question. Lament drew back and stared at him with little recognition, his gaze clouded. He rasped, "Asleep . . . feels like I'm still . . . dreamin' . . ."

"It's the flowers," Hellboy told him. "They're some kind of narcotic." He checked his belt, came up with a small first aid kit, and drew out some smelling salts. He shoved them under Lament's nostrils. "Here, this should help."

"What's that you say?"

"Come on, sniff these."

Lament did so and instantly revived. "Whew, lordy!"

As an afterthought Hellboy waved them under his own nose and was startled at how the acrid odor sobered him. He'd been a lot more out of it than he'd realized.

The atmosphere became palpable. They could both feel it, the afternoon darkening again with storm clouds moving in once more.

Every tap of branch against branch caused Hellboy to wheel, the wet mossbeards of cypress dripping and drawing his attention. The stink of death and rot flooded the area now that the women's alluring fragrance began to thin. He and Lament stood side by side, shoulder to shoulder, covering all directions.

"Feeling better?" he asked.

Nodding slowly, Lament said, "Greatly improved, thanks to your ministrations. My gratitude is stacking up to near chin-high right about now." He scanned the morass. "Watch yourself, there's still gators about."

"That's not the worst of our problems."

"Hardly ever is."

Lament stood with his arms out, hands open as if to make mystical gestures, in a stance Hellboy had seen sorcerers take many times before. He expected the hillbilly to start speaking in some unknowable language or hurl hexes from his fingertips.

But instead Lament simply shrugged out of his shirt and tore strips from the tail. He bound the deepest gash along his ribs, wincing as he knotted the rags around his chest. Hellboy still didn't understand what the guy was all about, but he had to let it slide. You could only cover so many things at once.

After tightening his bandage, Lament buttoned the remainder of his shirt back up, got his suspenders back on, and moved toward the paddies where the backwoods men lay in the watergrass.

"Them nasty critter-girls still nearby? Lord almighty, when they were on top of me I thought Sarah was among them. Saw her, even felt her . . . I could hear her voice deep inside me." The memory disturbed him and he shook his head to break free of it. "No wonder that crazy crippled ole coot didn't want us messin' with his dyin' comforts. I can understand it now."

"They're plants, grown over the remains of the dead," Hellboy explained, pointing to the remnants of the girlie whose head he'd crushed. "No, not plants, really . . . a single flora life-form that just appears to be many."

Lament kneeled and inspected the skeleton beneath the fibrous material. "Gator scratches and chew marks on the bone." He held the shredded tendril and examined the sap, which was pink from drawing blood from the men. Searching out Hellboy's eyes he said, "This whole area is a bad spot of swamp, but it's just as natural as any other. After the girlies have their supper, the gators come and clean the meat from the bones. Then, the plant life comes back and grows over the frame. A natural cycle. One hand washin' the other. It's beautiful in its own way."

"I'd call it a lot of things but 'beautiful' isn't one of them."

"You ain't from here," Lament said, moving to the men again.

"People from here don't seem to last long," Hellboy said.

"Granny Lewt near a hundred and sixteen." Lament stepped over some of the battered female husks. "Iffun these are just the buds . . . the leaves . . . the sweet meant to lure the prey . . . then where's the trunk of the thing?"

"Good question." Hellboy looked at the broken vines and followed them with his eyes as far as he could. Some had risen high over tree limbs and others went under the water, but they all ran into the deep scrub. He pointed. "That's where they went off, flying and dancing and floating." He cocked a thumb over his shoulder, pointing in the opposite direction. "So I guess we should go that way."

"'Ceptin' that's where we already come from."

"I was hoping you weren't going to tell me that."

Lament continued climbing through the knee-high water and finally reached the nest where the captured men from town lay. One after the other he found them in their rows, dead but grinning, propped up in their little patches of mud.

"I wonder if their loved ones would be thankful these boys all died so happy."

"I'm guessing not," Hellboy said. "A few of them were still alive a couple minutes ago."

They searched among the aisles, checking throats for pulses, turning over bodies mostly face-down in the shallows, but all the men were now lifeless.

"They been starved and drained," Lament told him.

"It wasn't just that," Hellboy said. A wave of guilt swept through him. The same way it had in Calcutta, Istanbul, and Beirut when the corpses lay scattered at his hooves. "I think it was the shock too. After the women left them they went into seizures, like addicts going cold turkey. I should've thought it through and been more careful."

"Not your fault, son. They were already too far gone. Even if any of them had survived this long, they woulda been as insane as that old man we run into, and destined to kill themselves anyways. Don't take on a burden that ain't yours to carry."

Hellboy wasn't salved, but he appreciated the words. "You know any of these guys?"

"No, but I suspect that Megan Dodd's husband Jorry is among them. The rest must be gator hunters, fur trappers, moonshiners, maybe some marijuana farmers. The mother plant must've started pluckin' at 'em one at a time at first, and then gathered more and more to it in recent days."

The brush rippled with breeze and Hellboy's shoulders tightened. Hot as it was, he was getting waterlogged and a chill worked through him. He snorted. "You got some really weird grannies around here if that's what they're growing back here. I always thought little old ladies liked chrysanthemums and tulips."

"I like to think she was fightin' it, tryin' to tame it. Granny witches are strong, nurturing women, they try to live in harmony with nature. It's what gives them their power."

"This isn't natural," Hellboy said.

Lament managed a chuckle. "It's a big odd world, son, or ain't you noticed?"

"All right, forget that. We've got to get the hell out of here. Where's the skiff?"

"Beached on gator ground or sunk most likely. We might have to slog our way out."

After all those miles traveled on the water through this emerald hell, the idea of trying to crawl out that same way made his tail twitch. "Is that even possible?"

"We'll know soon enough, I reckon. Unless we're lucky enough to run into Sarah out here, which is our whole purpose."

Hellboy thought it would be pretty damn humiliating to come this far to save three pregnant girls only to have to rely on them to walk him back home again.

"Come on now, let's get on our way," Lament said, and as he took a step away from the bodies and bones, the girlies burst from the tupelo scrub and catclaw brambles again and came hurtling forward. They swept down, diving and dancing.

"We've got to take this fight to them!" Hellboy shouted, preparing to club the women aside.

"No, that ain't the way," Lament told him. The women whirled and reached to hug him. "Do like I do, son. They ain't gonna stop until they woo us, so let them woo."

"Let them woo?"

"Yes. Have faith."

Instead of battling the beautiful feminine husks, Lament moved along with them across the shallows, easing himself one step at a time toward the deep wet scrub. The girls cooed and sighed and watched with black eyes, and Lament resisted while appearing to give in. He laughed with them. It was a sickening sound but it appeased the girlies. Hellboy marched along too, the women hanging onto him, their lips at his neck. He let them woo and they began to bleed him.

• • •

They tried to make Hellboy dance but he wouldn't dance. They tried to make him lie down at their knees but he wouldn't do that either. Lament seemed to be having fun, allowing them to literally sweep him off his feet. They lifted him to the trees and he glided around in the air, entwined by the soft pink arms of moss cultivated over gator-mauled skeletons.

Hellboy had to give it to him, he was a sharp little hillbilly, playing along like that. The girlies sipped at Lament's numerous small wounds but he didn't show any sign of pain. Instead he laughed like a gigolo and twirled among the fat tupelo leaves. The ladies responded with their tittering breaths from the boles.

The bizarre procession moved steadily through the jungle getting closer to the lair of the mother beast, whatever it might be. The vines grew taut and drew them in faster like a fisherman reeling in his lines.

Normally, walking into a head-on confrontation like this would only make Hellboy feel like an idiot, but he just didn't see any other way of getting on with his day.

Holding one of the women in his arms, hovering a few inches off the ground, Lament looked back over her shoulder at Hellboy and said, "Be on your toes, son. I mean your tippy-hooves. You feel it?"

"No."

"We're there."

And as they came up out of the scrub and weeds, they were. In a great wet tussock of bramble, chokeberry, lichen-covered oak, and mountainous logjam grew a mammoth tree that wasn't a tree. You could feel its antagonistic presence the way you could sense a furious man staring at the back of your head.

There was only a hint of a figure hidden among the reams of bark, branches, and seedling flora. You could just make out the shape of a colossal human being hunkered down in the mud, its limbs folded, hugging its knees to an immense torso. Its eyes were closed but the mouth was partially open and stuffed with flowers.

It looked to Hellboy like a sleeping woman.

Mama.

Why? he wondered. Why were the slumbering giants always the ones who caused such a goddamn ruckus?

Like waving hair on that massive being's head, the vines rose from the top of the Mother Tree and writhed in the air, some of the girlies suspended above while others lay in wait inside the enormous being's crevices and wrinkles. They laid out on the great wooden face sunning themselves, preparing to bloom. Dozens of the marionettes wafted about their mother, who had birthed them and raised them, and was them.

"Sweet Jesus at his loneliest hour . . ." breathed Lament. The ladies that held him, with their mouths red from the taste of his flesh, dropped him gently into the mud and floated off to join the others.

Hellboy shrugged off the husks still attached to his arms and chest and watched them flit away. "Guess that's Big Mama."

"I reckon so. Can you make out the web around her?"

Hellboy squinted and thought he saw, thanks to Granny Lewt's eyes, some kind of burning white filament about the Mother Tree. "That's a web? What kind of web?"

"A net of spells, set there by Granny Dodd, I s'pect. She knew enough to try to contain it and keep it from growing too wild. But when she died, the charms floundered. I still wonder if this was an entity she found here a'growin' or if she nurtured it for her own reasons."

"Does it matter?"

"I suppose not."

"I'm going to hit it."

Lament turned and looked at him. "Mayhap that's not the best course."

"And mayhap it is," Hellboy said. "That's what I do. I hit things and I hit them hard. If they get up I hit them some more. There's not much finesse, but it usually works." He tightened his hand into a fist, but that ethereal web glimmered again. "Unless you think you can strengthen the spells? Might give us an edge."

Palming away some blood on his neck, Lament shook his head. "Me? I done told you already, I don't know any magics."

"Right, I forgot. The magics know you."

"Say it with mistrust if you must, but it's the truth."

"I believe you," Hellboy said. "I don't understand it, but I believe you."

"Well, son, you're the one got yourself splinters of saints and all manners of inscribed silver trinkets. Can't you wield no enchantments?"

"No." Hellboy sighed and tried to figure out what the best way to go clobber a big sleeping tree woman might be.

The wind shifted and Lament covered his nose with his forearm, trying not to gag. Hellboy smelled it too, the narcotic perfume coming on strong. He turned away and got the smelling salts out again. He jammed them tightly to his nostrils and sniffed until tears squirted from his eyes.

When he spun back, Lament had gone down to one knee and was muttering to himself. "That fragrance again—urging free my dreams—I have dreams, you know, wonderful and plain, my wife on the porch, my child learning to sing—"

"Here, take the . . ."

"Wondrous, the places Mother takes you—"

" . . . smelling salts. Sniff them!"

Shaking his head to clear it, gritting his teeth and groaning, Lament managed to climb to his feet. "You keep them. I have something else."

From his pocket he drew out what looked like dried flowers. Again with the flowers, everywhere down here with the flowers.

All things being equal he'd rather be at the Brooklyn Botanical Gardens. Enough with the flowers. And the damn catfish.

Hellboy remembered Lament reaching for his pocket when they'd first come upon the nest. Lament placed the petals in his mouth and started to chew.

"What're those?"

"Roses. Held out to a woman who died a minute later, then placed on her grave in the sunrise."

"How are they supposed to help?"

"They've got power." He swept back his dirty wet hair, that scar on his scalp even more noticeable than before. It appeared to be much redder now, like a recent branding. "They were strewn on the floor and stained with her blood, so they're mighty bitter. They'll keep me focused."

Hellboy was going to ask more questions but figured it wasn't worth it. He just let the guy chow down. Besides, he couldn't argue with results. Lament's voice had lost that vacuous quality.

"So," Hellboy asked. "Where should I hit it? How do you kill a weed?"

"You scorch the earth," Lament said, and right then Mama opened her eyes.

CHAPTER 16

At least it appeared as if the mammoth Mother Tree opened an eye on its great feminine-like face, to now gaze at the intruders. Maybe it was just the shifting of leaves, but it sure looked like a seam in the bark had parted like an eyelid rising. The marionettes crowded around the massive trunk, dangling and waiting with the patience of the dead.

Lament said, "All right now, give me your lighter."

"How do you know I have a lighter? You're the one who fries turtle eggs."

"I only use wooden matches, and they're the very definition of soggified at the moment, son." He pointed at Hellboy's belt. "Looks like you got compartments a'plenty there. Ain't you got no fire?"

"I've always got fire," Hellboy said.

The girlies started to laugh and Lament turned, anxiety more deep-ly etched in his features.

"What is it?" Hellboy asked.

"The web is snapping loose. I don't know what's gonna happen next but it looks like Mama is waking up. We ain't got much time."

Hellboy grunted. They always started waking up right about at this point. The Goliath of Gol. The Baleside Behemoth. They'd be sleeping for millennia and twenty minutes after Hellboy showed up they'd be all quarrelsome and looking for trouble. It got a little depressing sometimes.

He reached into his belt and produced his Zippo. Its casing was dented from a couple of high-caliber bullets he'd taken in the chest a long time ago. He kept it mostly for sentimental reasons nowadays but it still worked. At least it had when he'd taken the skiff out and lit the lantern last night, before he'd spent the day fumbling around in all this muck.

"They say these things never fail. Let's see."

He snapped the Zippo open, sparked it by whipping it across the thigh that hadn't been mauled. It flamed immediately.

The girlies lifted on their vines and reeled away, mimicking human voices and making their chatter, waving their hands about their faces.

"They know to fear it," Lament said. "I reckon some of them moonshiners held on long enough to throw a burning sprig or two before they gave up the fight."

Hellboy grabbed hold for the nearest cluster of branches but the recent rains had wet them down too much. He pulled at the grass, grabbed hold of some of the thatching of briar. He pressed the lighter to it all but couldn't get anything other than a few puffs of smoke.

"The flame won't take, it's too wet here."

Hanging by their tendrils, the marionettes ceased their human-like activities at the same moment and froze in place. Limbs completely limp, eyes shut. Chins to their chests. At once they were all drawn to the top of the great Mother Tree's head, and lay flat against the bark, unmoving and forming a canopy of cover.

The earth began to stir and rumble, and the hummocks and thorny bushes swayed and then surged for the sky, the ground quaking and heaving.

"Aw crap, it can walk."

"Now that is a damn sight to behold."

Replacing the Zippo in his belt, Hellboy snarled, rushed forward, picked up speed, drew back his stone fist, and threw everything he had into punching big ole Mama in the knee. He connected powerfully and shouted, "How 'bout that!"

Not nearly enough. His fist barely scarred the bark. Mama had grown strong on the life-blood of so many men over the years.

It looked down at him. The ancient living eyes blinked at him, and the bellowed air seeped from a hundred knots in the tree, a desperate and vicious hiss of contempt escaping as Mama scowled.

"You done gone and riled her up somethin' fierce now!" Lament called.

"She pissed me off!"

"I done told you not to hit!"

"Yeah, well, maybe you were right after all."

Lament clucked as if about to castigate a child. Hellboy reached into his belt and found a flashbang grenade shell for his demolished pistol.

When you threw a punch it was natural, everything else was a pain. They'd told him the gun would fire even underwater. That it was self-cleaning and wouldn't ever gum up. Well, so much for that.

He tried to recall if the shell had to be primed. He couldn't remember. It had been seven or eight years since he'd used the flashbang. Maybe it had been in Istanbul, or Norway. He really should start writing these things down and keeping a little notebook with him.

"Move off, I'll draw it away."

"You sure about that, son?"

"Hell no."

Mama looked back and forth between Lament and Hellboy and settled on Hellboy. Well, of course. It bent and started coming for him, its anger apparent even without any expression on that vague face. Its hair of women tangled and knotted now as it moved in, reaching with its colossal arms. With the sound of a thousand sighs, it brought a gargantuan fist down.

Hellboy dodged. He lashed out and struck one of its giant fingers, and with a heartening crash he felt the wood give way and pulp beneath his fist. The huge tree limb acting as Mama's pinky sheared loose, fell, and stabbed into the soft earth. It teetered for a moment, and then toppled like an oak tree. Maybe it was an oak tree.

Mama's eyes bled a strange crimson sap and the eerie wheezing grew even louder. It bent lower, seeking Hellboy out, and prepared to smash at him again.

He shouted, "Lament, cover your ears and shut your eyes! Turn away!"

Hellboy drew out the shell, held it in his stone fist, and started to squeeze. He swung his hand into the face of Mama, who stared at him like it knew his name, had always known his name, and that no matter what happened next it would continue coming after him for the rest of his life. Maybe it was true. You could never tell.

Mama had a mouth after all. A huge cavity opened and out spilled more blood-colored sap and a blizzard of lethal flowers. Then those bones too old and fractured to be used in its luring, female-like bait cascaded around him. The calcium and phosphates of the dead went into feeding the grand vegetation. Nothing was wasted. It sneered at him, and it was the scorn of power, of nature itself. Lament had been right. It really was beautiful in its own way.

The Mother Tree made to swallow Hellboy. He shoved his fist forward and kept squeezing until finally the grenade detonated.

Boom.

The world went white-hot.

A searing lick of golden-white light spiked and exploded in an insane roaring blast. Hellboy screamed and the concussive force threw him high against Mama's face. The bark of its forehead bled where he struck it. A ball of wildfire broke inside the Mother Tree's mouth and soon hurled heaping flame across the girlies lying atop its head.

Coiling billows of smoke heaved around them. Hellboy managed to peel himself off the great tree, and he fell into the mud.

Mama tore herself from her own roots and the earth erupted all around. Hellboy's hand was still on fire and he had to drive it down deep into the wet, black soil to put the flames out. He looked up and watched as the Mother Tree's head flared, all the vines and girlies catching fire and bursting into flame.

The mammoth creature turned and opened its mouth as if to scream, but all that came free was the sound of boiling sap and the crackle of burning timber.

Mama reared, the fiery husks of the flailing marionettes dropping through the dangling cypress like ignited streamers. They ruptured against the earth and all across the jungle. The Mother Tree wept gallons of red bubbling syrup and eventually lurched toward the water, halted in its tracks, began to split apart, and plummeted into pieces.

Burning, log-sized chunks of timber rained down. Lament shouted, "This way!" and Hellboy sprinted for cover, the boiling sap splashing across the area. An arcing spatter caught Hellboy across the legs and he groaned and went down. Lament rushed forward, got a hand on Hellboy's wrist, and tried to pull him along. A huge burning branch smacked Lament across the shoulders and threw him into the mire. Hellboy staggered up and dove after him.

They both hit the water hard, the fiery husks striking around them. Super-heated skulls and other bones rolled and hissed past, skimming the surface before sinking.

Unconscious, Lament began to sink into the slime. Hellboy struggled to him, swimming and crawling. The toppling wood caused huge waves to rise in the swamp water, pressing Hellboy back.

By the time he got to Lament, the hillbilly wasn't breathing. Hellboy dragged him up onto the shore, avoiding the clumps of burning timber, and began CPR in the mud.

Thirty seconds later Lament coughed a wad of black muck from his lungs.

He lay on his back breathing deeply, looked over Hellboy's shoulder, and said, "Day ain't even near over yet."

Hellboy turned, and that's when he saw the pumpkin-headed kid and the fishboy staring at him through a partition of smoking reeds.

CHAPTER 17

They had stobbed to the far side of the dark lake and were work-ing their way around inlets too shallow for the pole. It had rained briefly but the black clouds had quickly rushed across the sky as if with great intent. Deeter had his hands on the oars, careful of running atop gator ground and sinkholes. Duffy had just torn off a wad of chaw and was offering it to his brother when Jester let out a cry like a dying loon and both Ferris boys practically jumped out of the boat.

Jester shot straight up in his seat, standing there with his head thrown back and eyes wide, crying up to the sky the way their ma had when they'd used the ax handles to beat her to death. Ma with her mouth open and hissing all manner of vile words right up to her unholy departure. Brother Jester was now looking the same way with his muscles locked, his top lip skinned back to bare his teeth.

Deeter's first thought was that this was their chance to be free of the damn crazy preacher. If the lake had been a little deeper then who knows, maybe he would've run forward and cracked Jester across the head with an oar and thrown him from the skiff.

As things were though, he was much too afraid to make any kind of move except nervously hop from foot to foot, which caused the boat to rock wildly and froth the silt beneath them.

Duffy knew that his brother's gesturing meant Deeter was hesi-tating on some kind of stupid thought. He reached out to put a hand on Deeter's shoulder to calm him some. As he did, an explosion deep in the jungle blew timber and scrub high up across their line of sight. The breeze rose through the cypress and a ghastly, putrid smell wafted toward them.

"Lord almighty," Duffy said, "boiled radishes and cabbage!"

"You reckon one of them old stills back in the woods done blown up?" Deeter asked.

"Don't smell like it none."

Jester's demented howl grew louder. The Ferris boys watched him, unsure of what to do.

With sparks of energy drifting from Brother Jester's eyes and mouth and fingertips, and skipping across the blackwater, the preacher floated a few inches out of the skiff. His heels caught on the slats of the seat for a moment and then struck the gunwales as he climbed into the air with his teeth electrified.

Deeter whispered, "The devil is with us this day. He done paying us a mighty long visit."

"Mayhap you're right," Duffy said, his head cocked, almost entranced by the scene. "But we always known it was comin'."

"I reckon, but it don't salve my heart none."

"Salvin' hearts is the last thing on the devil's mind, I s'pect."

The strange lightning played havoc across the marsh prairies ahead. The swamp was smoking now. A whitish-gray haze crawled over everything.

Both Ferris boys covered their noses and mouths, the stink of death heavy in the air. The foggy fumes crept closer and reached across the bow of the skiff. Deeter and Duffy backed into one another and held there unmoving. They'd dumped quite a few old boys in the mud from time to time, but neither had ever smelled anything like this. Meanwhile, Brother Jester just kept hanging there above the boat, looking all prophetized and full of apocalyptic vision.

"Should we just wait?" Deeter asked. "I'm really hungering."

"How can you eat with that hell-broth reek all over the marsh?"

"I'm a little partial to boiled radishes myself."

Brother Jester's mangled voice came from some endless well inside him. And yet, somehow, it also sounded as though that ruination came from far off in several directions as the preacher began to speak. *"The mother dies without bearing any children. The seeds never taking root, the pollen too strange for the bitter soil. What grace is this? Where is the beauty promised by the land?"*

"What's he sayin' about his mama?" Deeter asked.

"I figure it ain't his own mama he talkin' about."

"He gonna come back down in the boat or he just gonna hover there like a wasp all day long? I don't see why we can't have no fritters and beans while we waitin'."

"Let's give him whatever time he needs," Duffy said. "I don't want him trackin' behind us if we go on our way. Man like that, he don't forget those that cross him."

"I remember his grievous touch, but I don't like bein' no man's drudge, 'specially if he don't even allow me to have no lunch when it's past midday. We got any jerky and biscuits left?"

"Forget that. Ain't much more to this venture so long as we find them girls today and attend them fellas. We be home by sunset."

"Iffun Preacher ever come on down from the mid-air."

"The mother burns and bubbles and boils." Jester went on. *"She who was alone and without any friend. She who did nothing except give. Give to the prey and give to the ground and water. There was love and kindness. And now only fire and splinter and ash. Whoever heard, whoever listens to the heartfelt plea, blight those that eradicate me. Do unto them as they have done. Burn them. Burn the children."*

With that Brother Jester's head slumped and he dropped back into the boat, the sparking display of power dwindling and going out. He landed so hard that the boat tipped hard to one side, and the twelve-gauge pump sloshed overboard. Deeter whispered, "Why that no good—"

"Hush," Duffy told him. "We still got Plume Wallace's weapon."

"A damn double-barrel instead of a pump."

"I'll get you a new one fer yer birthday."

"You will?"

"Iffun we live to see the day."

Jester sat there in the stern, his eyes full of terrible thoughts. The Ferris boys waited. They chawed their chaw and spit into the water. Deeter's stomach rumbled. The smoke drifted out of the deep brush and across the waterways.

Shadows wreathed Jester, within and without, his body and soul, and they told him how the destructive hand of his hellish enemy had murdered a strange and unique being out in the greenery.

Its death throes continued to send harrowing shockwaves through the mystical currents that Jester was privy to. Its dying petitions assailed and besieged him. Ivory as his skin was, it paled further.

He had not felt such a strong sense of sorrow and faithlessness since his own death.

His archangel shadows offered bits of knowledge about the great mother, now dead, and the swamp was more desolate for it. He was mournful that they had not been faster today. The murder might have been averted, the mother saved, the lonely men attended and set free upon the backs of seraphim.

"You all right, Preacher?" Duffy ventured. "What was all that caterwaulin' about?"

"Row us out of here."

Deeter sat and took the oars again. "Iffun you say." He kept to the same course, which would lead to the tussocks and the mired shore where all the smoke seemed to come from.

"No," Jester said. "Not that way. Take the other inlet." Pointing with a claw-like finger. "There, you see."

"Why that one?" Duffy said. "It ain't nothin' much but a creek."

Jester looked at him. "It is where we wish to go."

"Well, that'll learn me for ponderin' on a foolish question."

Deeter rowed them over the shallows and into a new channel

that brought the skiff to thinner tracks of tattered pine. Timber wolves prowled in the lightwood, their eyes anxious in the underbrush. Duffy took to stobbing again and Deeter angrily picked up the double-barrel shotgun. They might run aground on a sandbar and the wolves, though fearing man, might still take a run at them.

The emerald thickness around them fell away as they passed more hummocks. Bull gators in the distance roared and tore up the stillness of the late afternoon.

"It brings us to the women," Jester said, grinning. "To my Sarah. And her child."

Duffy worked the stobpole, easing it free from jetsam and occasional logjam. "And what we gonna do when we get there, Preacher, if you don't mind me askin'?"

"You'll do as you're intended to do."

Deeter spit some chaw. "And for me and my brother, those intentions in this case might be what . . . ?"

"Well . . . murder, Deeter," Jester the walking darkness said, his teeth burning. "Whatever else are you good for except murder?"

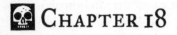 Chapter 18

The ill children led Hellboy and Lament through the scrub, hopefully toward the swamp village. The pumpkin-headed kid, the kid with eyes like an insect, the beautiful girl without bones in her legs who rode on Lament's shoulders, the dwarf with the big feet, the really weird conjoined twins who had two legs, two arms, and two heads, and Fishboy Lenny.

It made for a heck of a troupe, all of them moving through the marshy woodland together like some bizarre grade-school field trip. The oddest part of the whole situation was perhaps how familiar and natural this course felt to Hellboy, as if it had always been meant for him to be here.

Despite their appearance the children acted like you'd expect any happy children to behave. They chased each other through the cabbage palms and slough, their laughter echoing across the green. They bumped their heads and scuffed their knees and cried, then shake it off and forget about it.

They were so used to the semi-solid, soft ground that they hardly threw any mud as they went by. They moved with ease through the runty bay bushes and matted catclaw thickets. They slithered and hopped, bounded and rollicked, and kept up a steady stream of patter in what sounded like a half-dozen different languages. Granny Lewt's ears weren't helping him at all with understanding any of them, and he was wondering if the magic might be wearing off a little by now.

Luckily Fishboy Lenny didn't happen to look like a catfish. Hellboy was thankful for small graces, thinking, Jesus, no more catfish for the time being, all right? The kid just looked like your *average* fish, with flippers instead of hands, two slashes of nostrils where a nose ought to be, and a mouth that was hardly more than a small hole through which he made lots of happy noises. The boy also had vestigial gills just under his shrunken ears.

Fishboy Lenny's name was the only one he'd managed to catch, although all the kids had introduced themselves. But Lenny, he just swept up through the mud and said, "Fweep mwah fsshhh. Lenny." So there it was.

Every now and again one of the kids would turn back to Hellboy and playfully grab his hand, trying to get him to move along a little faster.

But he didn't feel all that hot to trot at the moment and Lament looked even worse. The hillbilly's hair was singed, his wounds still bled a bit, and he had welts across his face and burns on his arms and hands. None of it slowed him up much though, and he pulled out his mouth-harp and started to play a tune.

The girl on Lament's shoulders knew the song and began to sing, keeping time by tapping at his chest with her soft unformed feet. Soon the rest of the children joined in on the lilting melody. Hellboy didn't understand the words at all.

When Lament finished and put his mouth-harp back in his pocket, the girl gestured to be let down. Hellboy lifted her off Lament's back and put her on the ground, where she swung herself along wriggling and using her arms as crutches. Soon the pumpkin-headed kid and the kid with insectoid eyes each gripped one of her hands and carried her between them.

Lament stopped and threw a shoulder against a hurrah bush, breathing sharply. Hellboy asked him, "You need a rest?"

"I could use hot meal," Lament said, "a bubblebath, a lengthy foot massage, a long drink of moon, some dry long johns, and a warm downy bed, but even without them kind privileges I s'pect I'll survive." He turned and smiled. "How you holdin' up, son? Wishin' you'd never had no truck with us southern folk?"

"I've had a lot of truck with southern folk before," Hellboy told him, "but none of that trucking ever turned out quite like this."

"Make your memoirs interesting though."

They trudged on. They'd already walked at least a couple of miles, and Hellboy kept wondering about the kids' parents, if they'd be worried. They had to be, right? If all the noise and fire and smoke hadn't drawn them out to the Mother Tree, there still would've been a chance they'd wound up on gator ground or in some other kind of trouble. Lost in the woods, attacked by wolves, bitten by snakes. He mulled and started to brood a touch.

Lament picked up on it right away. "What's the matter with you?"

"What are they doing out so far from home?"

"What do you mean? This is home. They were just playin'."

"What were they doing out there by the flats?"

"They heard tell that some swamp men got drawn away from their homes and decided to take a looksee for themselves. No child can resist a good mystery."

"They could've been hurt."

Nodding, Lament said, "Coulda been killed. No different than a city child walkin' home from school, I reckon."

"I'm not so sure about that."

But of course he was. He'd been in the Syrian desert with kids only a little older than these who'd been his contacts and guides. He'd seen children playing in bombed out cars in Beirut. He'd once visited a monastery in China and met with a ten-year-old Buddhist abbot whose only purpose in life, along with his brotherhood, was to recite one hundred million prayers to hold back the undoing of all creation. He'd met a lot of kids who had been put into the thick of things.

"What's really on your mind, son?" Lament asked.

Good question. Hellboy glanced at the kids and could almost see how it would be if they ever decided to leave their swamp village. The prejudices they'd face. The pain of not fitting in. Even if you didn't want to fit in, even if nobody else needed you to fit in with them. The kids were oblivious now, but they wouldn't always be. It struck him deep, knowing what it would be like for them eventually.

Hellboy hissed something and Lament said, "What's that?"

"How's this happen?" Hellboy repeated. "How does something like this happen?"

"How's what happen?"

"*This.*"

With a little heat in his voice, Lament said, "You think you got the bloom on strange births?"

"I didn't say that."

"No, you didn't. The Lord don't differentiate between the unsightly and the adorable. We're all born under Heaven. We're all God's children, every one of us, you never heard that before?"

"I've heard it," Hellboy said, his hooves sinking deep in the muck, and thinking Lament might just be a little on the stupid side after all. "Never figured it applied to me."

"Oh, you're just feelin' a touch of melancholia. That's natural enough after the day we've had, for a man far from home. The world is full of odd beauty. I already done told you that, iffun you recall. No different here than anywhere." They marched along and, after a while, Lament went on. "I'm sorry, son, I shouldn't have snapped at you like that. How's this happen? You can have your pick of answers. There's plenty of them. Maybe none are true or maybe all of 'em are."

"I wasn't really asking. It was rhetorical. I know about mutations."

Lament's face hardened. "Maybe you only think you do. Got your mind set on poisoned moonshine and improperly buried bodies during epidemics, don't ya? Or we can talk about all the toxic waste dumping going on. I seen them chemical polluters myself, throwing in barrel after barrel. I fought 'em off with fists and a good hunk'a chicory. Men from the town kept a watchful eye for a year or two, and sent some of them boys runnin' with their keesters full of buckshot. But I don't know that it ever stopped them. There's too much money to be saved dumpin' into these depths. Corporations aren't always righteous. Nor the government."

Hellboy, who'd been a part of the government practically since he was born, said nothing.

"And the granny witches," Lament went on, "they say there's ancient forces in the blackwater, and you and I know that's true. Whether said evils reach into the blood of men and women to affect the children or not, I guess everyone has their own say about that."

Putting it like that, Hellboy wondered exactly how it was that all these people weren't on the verge of mutation or cancerous illness or zombification.

"The real question is, why you askin' the question at'all?"

"I don't know."

"Yeah, you do. You thinkin' about family."

"I don't think about family. Ever."

"Iffun you say."

Far ahead, the pumpkin-headed boy turned and rushed back, excitedly chattering to Hellboy although Hellboy couldn't understand him. Lament would have to translate.

"Enoch says we're almost there."

"That's his name? Enoch?"

"It's biblical."

"I know it's biblical. How is it you can speak their languages?"

"They just speakin' English, as well as they can manage it."

Fishboy Lenny went, "Fweep mwash. Wooph."

Hellboy said, "I can't understand a word of it."

"Neither can I."

"You don't know the language, the language knows you."

Lament let out a smile. "That's right, son. Now we're con-fabulatin'."

An ugly thought struck Hellboy and he stopped short. "Hey, these swamp people, they're not luring these teenage girls here with their babies to try to bring new blood to the people, are they?"

"Why'd they want to go and do that?"

"To clean up the gene pool."

Lament frowned, scratched at the scabbing wound on his neck, and looked at Hellboy for a long time. Enoch stepped up, leaned toward Lament's ear, and let loose with a stream of quiet gibber-ish. Lament listened and nodded, and finally went, "Oh, now I see. Thank ya."

"What was that about?" Hellboy asked.

"Oh, he was just explainin' to me what it was you meant." La-ment blinked at Hellboy. "You got yourself a complex mind, son, you truly have. The answer is no, the babies ain't here for no ge-netic purposes."

"Well, good."

The kids climbed over a sycamore log in the brush upsetting bitterns, limpkins, and squawk herons. There was a quick flutter of many wings and a rush through the leaves. The land gave way to more solid soil littered with clumps of palmettos, oak, and palm trees.

"You sure this is the right way?" Hellboy asked.

"I've never lost myself quite this badly before. So no, I ain't sure of much at the moment. But the children, they know. So long as we follow, we'll get to the village soon enough."

"I still don't get why Sarah came all this way. What's so safe about this place?"

"Prayers and will have power. This was once a shanty town where the swamp folk held their all-night sings. A lot of healin' and good will and faith and miracles took place on this ground. Suppose it's about as holy a spot as you're likely to find anywhere near Enigma."

"And yet it's where all these poor people live now. The ground hasn't done much to make them well."

"Depends on whether you think they're sick, I reckon. Do you?"

"I didn't say that—"

"It's all right, son, I know what your intent was. You just need to understand that what some folks might call freaks, others consider blessed."

"I think I understand that pretty damn well."

"See that then? Already you better off than a whole slew of ignorant dullards."

"That makes me feel a lot better."

"Good. Always glad to help a friend."

It began to rain lightly and the kids all let out whoops of joy. Hellboy didn't quite get it, but he liked that they were so full of energy and elation. He hoped they stayed here in their little corner of the planet, where they might count on one another and their people to get them through. The rest of the world would try to steal that laughter from them.

Passing beneath a sharp palmetto frond he felt something cold brush against his cheek. He looked up and a huge snake was hanging uncoiled from the leaves, its mouth open.

Hellboy shoved Lament aside. "Watch it . . . a snake!" He brought his stone hand up and caught the snake just as it was prepared to leap.

Lament said, "It's only a timber rattler."

"Only a rattler?"

"At least it ain't a cottonwood mocassin. Just don't let it bite you. Go on and let it get about on its way."

"Oh." Hellboy opened his fist. The rattler wasn't about to ever get about on its way again.

"I don't think you needed to squeeze it quite so hard, son," Lament told him.

"Guess I overreacted a bit."

The kid with the insectoid eyes came running over and asked Hellboy in perfectly nuanced English, "Are you plannin' to keep it?"

"I hadn't thought about it."

"May I have it, please?"

"You want a crushed dead snake, kid?"

The boy nodded enthusiastically. "Yes, please."

Shrugging, Hellboy figured, All right, whatever. He handed the timber rattler to the kid, who grinned, and the snake was reflected and refracted about a billion times in his eyes. The boy ran off to rejoin the others ahead.

A few years back Hellboy had run into a cult of Nyarlothepian sorcerers down in Paraguay who used boiling baths of serpent venom to call up long-slumbering demi-gods. Now he couldn't even go to the reptile cages at the Bronx zoo without thinking about bad juju.

"What's he want with the snake?" Hellboy asked, wiping his hand clean on a thatch of fronds.

Lament said, "Well, it ain't for no damn genetic purposes, if you still got that on your mind. Why else would he want it? It's 'cause he's hungry."

"He's going to eat it?"

"Probably bringin' it back to his ma so she can fricassee it and feed it to the whole family. They make for good eatin', especially with fried rice."

"Jesus Christ."

"Can't exactly order in prime rib and chicken cacciatore out this far in the bogland. Can't order it in town neither, but that's another matter altogether. Folks here live on snake and lizard, gator meat, wild goat, hog, duck, squirrel, and fish, mostly."

For years Hellboy had been so busy fighting the infernal orders, the angry dead, the towering trolls, ogres, and dragons that he sometimes forgot there were simpler issues abounding. Like sick kids without bread. He had to stay hooked in to the world. It was easy to get too caught up in paranormal events and forget about the orphans.

Hellboy heard music in the distance. The children grew excited and rushed along faster toward the sound. Hellboy reached down and lifted Fishboy Lenny, hoping to put the kid up on his shoulder the way Lament had carried the girl, but the little fishy guy just slipped out of Hellboy's grasp and squirmed away.

So much for that.

Lament said, "Well, I think we're nearly there. Lord help us if Sarah and the girls ain't. I'm not sure where to search next."

"We'll find them, don't worry. You've been to this village before. What's it like?"

"They were glorious times. I was a young'n and still sang the gospel. Used to have all-night sings out this way. People'd come in from as far as three hundred miles to listen and bear witness."

"Listen to you and Jester."

His eyes clouding, Lament nodded. "Wasn't much of a town at the time, nor populated by so many people with special consideration under the Lord. But it was here." He watched the girl with no bones in her legs slither along in the cabbage leaves. "I seen my share of one-of-a-kind peoples in my travels, same as you have. Some good, some not so good. The more different we are from one another, the more the same I discover us to be. Sharing problems and fears and endeavors. Not any one of us is so strange as to not have the same hopes and heartaches, not even you, I reckon."

"How about Jester?"

"He's not all that different from the rest of us neither," Lament said, brushing his wet hair from his face. "Except he's dead and won't lay down."

"That could be considered a pretty big difference."

"I'm not so sure."

The pumpkin-headed kid let out a holler. Fishboy Lenny returned to Hellboy and went, "Fweep," and then scurried off again. Breaking clear of the brush now Hellboy saw clusters of paintless cabins and crescent rows of dark shanties lining the slopes of slough, vine-draped and overgrown with hanging orchids. The music grew louder. Fiddles, banjos, washboards, and squeezeboxes wheezed and rattled and twanged out.

It was a hell of a racket, and yet just as with Lament's tunes, Hellboy felt himself willing to go with it. A couple of screen doors clattered in the hot breeze. He thought they must've been having one of their swamp weddings or revivals out in the bog, despite the rain. Or maybe not. Maybe they were just enjoying life.

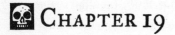# CHAPTER 19

People walked up and greeted them, making a fuss, calling for a doctor, and offering skins of clean water, wine, and whiskey.

Hellboy gulped down two bags of water, hardly taking a breath between them. Weird to think this place with so much marsh and quagmire and rain would make him as dry as if he'd crossed the Kara Kum desert. It wasn't an exaggeration. He'd crossed the Kara Kum desert once, and this was worse.

He was surprised at the size of the town. Someone mentions a swamp village you think maybe seven or eight shacks, a handful of folks carving out some kind of hardscrabble life. But as he looked about he saw more and more buildings in the distance, larger homes, a kind of main street with stores on it. The hum of gas-run generators thrummed beneath all the other noise.

The channels of swamp water ran between houses, and small bridges had been built to span them. There were stables, chicken coops, and barns. He saw goats and pigs in small corrals. Several skiffs sat at the sycamore-lined bank of a large creek that led back into the deeper bog.

Teens fished beside their fathers. He saw tots pushed along in babycarts. This was a true community, as real as any other town he'd been in, and he knew without asking that it had no name.

When he was sated he turned and saw people still scuttling around Lament, who was lying on a cushioned bench on a nearby veranda. An old white-haired man with a bushy silver mustache and thick glasses, who actually looked like a small-town doctor, turned out to be a small-town doctor. He even carried a black bag. His shirt was buttoned to the collar and he wore a string tie and walked through the crowd with an air of controlled annoyance. When he reached Lament the doc immediately began to examine him.

"Quit makin' such a bother over me," Lament said, "I tell you I'm all right."

"Hush now, we all got our chores to attend and jobs to do. So let me do mine."

"Forget that. Is Sarah here? Tell me she's here."

"She is, and she's fine, so now you just settle yourself."

"I need to see her!"

The old man cleaned his glasses with the ends of his tie. "If you want to see Sarah again you'll hold still. You've got a broken rib poised to enter your lung, and you must've dropped two or three pints of blood already."

"Oh, that ain't so much."

"It ain't much when you're drinking moonshine, but it's plenty to lose from your pulmonary system. You're a mass of lacerations, abrasions, contusions, acute edema, hairline fractures, and exhaustion."

"You just like haulin' out fancy words."

"Hush and lie back or I'm a'gonna conk you with a rock."

Lament lay down and allowed the doc to do his work. Hellboy wasn't sure what he'd been expecting the old man to pull from his bag, maybe leeches and mud packs, eyes of newt and a jar labeled *Doc's Gallbladder*, but he was impressed when he saw the doc filling a needle with antibiotics. Afterward, he used a staple gun to close Lament's gator scratches and other wounds, and bandaged the busted ribs.

The doc washed his hands in a metal bowl and pointed at Hellboy. "You next, friend."

"I'm okay."

Doc sighed, threw back his head, and stared at the heavens. "Lord save me from such hardheaded, steely roughnecks." He glowered at Hellboy. "Son, my name's Doc Wayburn. I'm seventy-one years old and I can measure out with a yardstick the distance I've got left before I reach the Elysian Fields. You gonna make me waste my precious remaining days arguing with you too?"

Hellboy was more afraid of the old guy conking him with a rock. "Okay, I'll settle in and try to be a good patient."

He sat beside Lament on the bench and Doc Wayburn inspected his wounds, gingerly removing the torn strips of his coat and prodding here and there.

"You a veteran, son?" the doc asked.

"What makes you say that?"

"These are field dressings. Nicely done too. You been on the battleground."

"I've seen my share of scrapes."

"Of that I'm sure, son."

Doc Wayburn continued his ministrations, taking care of the wounds, dressing and suturing a few injuries Hellboy hadn't even been aware of, considering how battered he was. His left hoof had cracked at the edge, and the doc ran off to a nearby home and returned with a petroleum-based sealant. He said, "It'll take a few months for the split to grow out. Until then, you might consider shoeing it to keep the crack from getting worse. We got a good old boy blacksmith can fix that right up."

"Thanks for your help, I'll be fine."

"As you say, then. I got some more rounds to make." And with that he smoothed down his thick mustache and marched off through town.

The children brought plates of food and Lament and Hellboy sat side by side on the veranda, tired and neatly bandaged, eating and drinking wine. Hellboy didn't know what was on his plate and he was glad nobody told him. He wasn't about to ask.

"Doc Wayburn told me Sarah's fine," Lament said.

"I heard. That's good. Where is she?"

"I don't know, but if she don't show up in the next few minutes I'm a'gonna go lookin'."

A couple more people came up and said hello to Lament, treating him with some reverence, even celebrity. When they'd gone Hellboy said, "I thought you hadn't been here since you were a boy."

"I haven't."

"Then how do they all know you?"

"Some know your name too. You gonna ask them about that as well?"

Hellboy figured that he'd made the papers at least a couple of times even down here. "That's different."

"Mayhap."

"Enough with the mayhaps already."

"I know a good many of these folk from Enigma. Some of 'em have, ah, retired from town life and come out here to live. Others come because of their children. Some you might say commute between Enigma and the village. And some, well, you know—"

"I know? What do I know?"

Lament said, "Some I know from my dreams."

The children began to dance again, and the folk returned to their food and their music. Who knew a washboard and an empty jug and three strings drawn up a broom handle could create such complete and rich songs? More clapboard doors clattered in the wind. The air was full of laughter. Fishboy Lenny just hung in the background, waving his flippers. Hellboy waved back and the kid spun in happy circles.

Hellboy looked closely at the people, seeing the slight mutations in many of them. He saw webbed hands and vestigial gills in several people. Others who had animal-like, reptilian, or insectoid features. Maybe their mutations were just a leap in genetic adaptation to their swampy surroundings.

Pointing up the main street, he said to Lament, "I'm going to take a look around this way."

"I think I'll head in the other direction. Give a shout if you run into any more mischief. It'll be getting dark soon."

With that they stood and began to move off, Hellboy thinking maybe Fishboy Lenny could lead him around the town, show him the sights, the corn crib and the place where they shucked oysters or caught crawfish, or whatever it was that they did, but before he took two steps Lament gripped his elbow. "Hold on, son. Town elder is a'comin'."

"Who would that be?"

"This here would be Granny McCulver."

Hellboy thought, Well sure, of course, another granny. What else had he been expecting?

This granny was a hell of a lot different from Granny Lewt, that was for certain. She was young and a stone knockout. She had all her limbs and features. As she moved among her people, the crowd parted to let her by. The music rose and the song grew in strength. He felt the pleasant pressure of her power exerting itself. The great force of her character.

He didn't know where the granny part came into it at all—she looked about thirty on the outside. A very fine and well-endowed thirty. He couldn't figure out exactly how she'd made it to granny status, but decided to put off the question as he stared.

"Son, your tongue is danglin'," Lament said.

"Oh boy."

Her glossy, lustrous black hair fell about her shoulders and swirled in the breeze. Eyes like burnished black diamonds were emphasized even more by her pale, heart-shaped face. She grinned with slightly parted rose-petal lips, her perfect white teeth shining through.

The pumpkin-headed kid stood nearby and smiled so widely, with his head tipped to one side, that he nearly fell over. She patted the little tuft of hair at the top of his dome and the kid swooned. Hellboy didn't blame him.

He breathed, "Wow."

She strode up and said, "John Lament, we welcome you to our village once more, and your friend as well. It's been some time since you've visited, and quite a changed sight this must be for you."

With a little nod of deference, Lament said, "Ma'am McCulver, nice to see you again."

Hellboy figured he'd just follow the routine. He nodded too, as in, yep, yep, well all righty then, and said, "Ma'am McCulver, how's it going?"

Lament stood there like he might be poised for anything, the hinges of his jaw tight and pulsing, and she said, "Ease your mind, John, Sarah and her two companions are at my home, resting."

Lament actually slumped and Hellboy had to reach out to keep him from falling. "Thank the Lord."

"They arrived last night, in the dark without hardly any moon. She found her way here because she was meant to. Becky Sue Cabbot was with her, ready to burst, and round about sunup she gave birth to a lovely baby girl. But Sarah and young Hortense—"

Hellboy thought, Hortense, ah jeez . . .

"—Millford, they're still holding on, though it won't be long now."

But Hellboy realized girls named Hortense, they were made of stern stuff. For her to have come through that slough, all this way, heavy with child, it brought his chin up in respect.

The rain began again, a slight drizzle that no one acknowledged, not even Hellboy who was getting used to it. Ma'am McCulver brushed a hand across her forehead and drew her hair to the side, and her force and beauty radiated even more strongly. He wondered if it was a bewitching, if he was really staring at some century-old hag trying to pull a fast one. He had charms that might break the illusion if there was one, but he decided, Why make life even tougher?

"Tell me what happened out there," she said. "I know the blackwater has been restless and a'grieved, the land agitated lately. I heard screaming and terrible crying at the rim of my ear, and a voice begging to burn away the children. Tell me, which children are in danger?"

Lament related the story of the Mother Tree and Mama's girlies. "It wasn't what I wanted, but we had no choice. There are fields of dead men out there in the wet grasses."

"Lord, if only I'd known about it sooner, but I've been distracted with events here. Since my sister's passing, I've struggled with new responsibilities. The town's growing faster than we can handle. Our numbers have become so inflated, even though so many of our kin have gone missing these last few weeks."

"A good many of them won't be returnin'."

"If only I'd been paying greater attention," she said, her lovely face folding into grimness. "But village concerns draw me from my leanings, the ways of my mothers and sisters. We're having this celebration to remind us of all we have, and to fight our growing despair."

"And to protect yourselves. The music has charms."

"Yes. The walking darkness approaches. I sense it. And times have grown rougher these past few years. The chemical dumping is becoming worse all the time. Too much time is spent in Enigma barring roads and keeping a lookout for the trucks. The soil and river fights us more and more. There's less fish. The gator poachers kill off whole strains."

Hellboy said, "I might be able to help."

"How?"

"I can make a call."

Ma'am McCulver didn't seem to understand. "Call? Call whom?"

"I work for some people who have pull. We'll track it down. I'll do my best make it stop."

"They won't stop, they'll simply go elsewhere. Another corner of a different swamp."

He shrugged. "You're probably right," he admitted, "but we do what we can, right?"

Still, she smiled and said, "I hear the deep truth in your voice. Thank you for your willingness to aid us."

"Sure."

Pushed to his very edge, Lament said, "I need to see Sarah."

"Of course," the gorgeous granny told him, "I'll take you to her."

In the soft rain, they walked the length of the village past cabins, pinewood shacks, and tin-roofed sheds. Several of the children came along, including the pumpkin-headed kid and Fishboy Lenny, who murmured and muttered together, occasionally laughing.

Led by Ma'am McCulver, the party moved steadily toward a three-story, coffee-colored house in the distance. Hellboy heard babies crying again, sometimes in his ears and sometimes, it felt like, at the back of his head. The granny woman glanced his way from time to time, smiling vaguely.

As they approached her home he saw it had a whitewashed wraparound veranda bordered by palm trees and sugarcane. Three teenage girls sat out on porch swing cut from fresh pine. One held a baby in her arms. Lament's step began to speed up until he was almost running. Losing a few pints of blood didn't mean much in the face of love. One of the pregnant girls broke from the others and moved to meet him.

So this was Sarah.

He could see touches of Bliss Nail in her right off. The same steel-gray eyes full of tenacious strength, unyielding and with a hint of defiance in even her most modest gestures. She wasn't exactly what you'd call beautiful, but there was an attractive and compelling earthiness to her that really struck him.

"I know, I've had my share as well."

"But mine . . . the baby. I woke two nights ago and found a pair of bullfrogs on my belly croakin' together. I fear. I fear a'mighty."

"Don't . . . it's gonna be all right. Whatever happens, it's the Lord's will and we'll trust in that."

Hellboy wondered if he should talk about his own dream last night, except he couldn't remember what it was about. But it had been there and it had meant something.

The pumpkin-headed kid loped up onto the porch out of the drizzle and the others followed. He bent and made faces at Becky Sue Cabbot's newborn. Hellboy was introduced to her and Hortense Millford, two stern-faced, sunburned, tired-looking young women, one of whom had just delivered a child and the other close to bearing her own.

The music from the other end of the village drifted in and brought with it a sense of solace. Now Hellboy knew what Lament had meant when he said the music had charms. The songs were spells of protection. Just because Ma'am McCulver was easy on the eyes didn't mean she didn't know a little something about spellcasting.

They moved into the house and he was a bit surprised to see it was sparsely decorated, without all the batwings, frogs' tongues, bubbling cauldrons, and magical potions of Granny Lewt's home.

More thunder groaned. He thought that whatever was going to happen would have to happen soon. That was just the way of these things. Ma'am McCulver gave him the look again and this time he stared back. There was a humanity and sadness in her eyes that worked its way into his chest.

Suddenly Sarah's face twisted as if in pain, and her back straightened. She hissed through her teeth and reached out to grip Lament's arm. He held onto her tightly.

"It's startin'," she said.

"Now?" Lament asked, then frowned that he'd say such an asinine thing. But it was a father's prerogative to be a little dopey when his kid was being born.

"Contractions. Damn, that felt odd. Not sure what I was expectin' but I wasn't expectin' that."

Sometimes you were glad when you were proven right and sometimes you weren't. Hellboy thought, Yeah, the kid's got to come along just before the big beat down.

He said, "Take her to the bedroom. Stay with her." He told the pumpkin-headed kid, "You, think you could go get Doc Wayburn?"

The boy nodded eagerly and took off through the village.

Hellboy asked, "Which way do you think Jester will be coming from?"

"Most probably the creek," Ma'am McCulver said, pointing. "It connects to the river. It isn't an easy pass, but if he remembers his way, that's how he'll come."

"It's getting dark and the storm's about the break over us. It's been my experience that that's when the trouble usually hits. I'm going to go see what I can see."

Torn by responsibility, Lament's eyes filled with concern. "You're gonna need my help."

He was ready to leave his girl. For the good of the rest of them. Jesus, the guy had heart. Hellboy said, "You stay here. Don't do anything crazy."

"You ain't seen crazy yet, son."

"Let me handle it."

"You? That's my true foe. Why'm I gonna let you handle it?"

"I've been doing this a long time. I can handle myself. You just watch over your girlfriend and your baby. That's what this is about, remember?"

With a bleak expression, Lament narrowed his eyes. Hellboy laid a hand on his shoulder and said, "Trust me."

"I do."

"Well, all right then."

All the tension seemed to snap from Lament then. "Don't forget, he's got the Ferris boys with him. Don't be fooled by their graceful features, they're killers."

"If it's one thing I'm not fooled by, it's graceful features."

"So you say."

Sarah, struggling to mask her pain, said, "The Ferris boys comin' here too?"

"Yeah, he roped them in."

They exchanged a glance heavy with meaning.

Fishboy Lenny went, "Fweep mwash. Wooph."

Ma'am McCulver said, "I wish to help but I'll be unable to do so." She stared out the window at the brush, the land, the homes. "He performed miracles here. He saved lives. He healed the ill, the crippled, the blind. He brought God down to us when the Lord did not listen to us. And since then the divine has not left us. The very land itself owes him. Do you understand?"

Hellboy shook his head. "No."

"My sisters and I have always been a part of the swamp. We can effect little change on its nature, on the things that it wants."

"Things that the swamp wants?"

"Yes. We help where we can but we are, like all, merely slaves to the greater forces about us."

He didn't quite understand, but enchantresses and goblin kings and trolls often talked like this. Even Lament did it, saying how the magic knew him. Sometimes you just had to nod and go forward on your own. Most of the time, in fact.

Hellboy started for the door but the granny witch stepped in front of him, blocking his way. She leaned forward and he expected maybe a kiss for his troubles, which would've been just fine under the circumstances.

"Hold still," she said.

"What is it?"

When her hands touched him he watched as a black spark skittered across his stone fist. There was nothing to it, he felt no different at all, but in the light of the setting sun he could see a shadow slowly making its way over the ridge of his knuckles. He didn't know what that meant but it couldn't be good. He plucked at it and couldn't touch it. Ma'am McCulver, though, snatched at it and somehow got a grip. She tugged at the small piece of darkness and tore it from Hellboy. She held it in her pale hand where it coursed across her fingers, tame and almost loving.

"I dreamt of shadows," Hellboy said, remembering.

"And they dream of you," she told him. "The night's nearly upon us. Jester will arrive soon."

"He's already here," Fishboy Lenny said. Then, "Fwashh fweep!"

CHAPTER 20

Deeter checked the load in Plume Wallace's shotgun and said, "I hear music. Goddamn, that boy sure can play a jug. You listenin' to that?"

"I am," Duffy said, dragging the skiff up onto the creek bank. "It's some fine banjo-playin' and squeezeboxin' too."

"As good as Pa used to play."

"Better'n him, I reckon. Better'n him before his third or fourth tap of moon anyways. Pa always improved as the night went on."

Brother Jester, pressing through the palmettos, allowed the magics of the music to rake against him like barbed wire. He grunted, enjoying the raw ache, and said, "It's a powerful charm, a circle of peace and protection. Harmonies of the heavens, it lures even the angels astray."

The Ferris boys stared at one another, then down into the mud and around at the wet brush, looking for circles and seeing none. Deeter placed a hand on the sheathed Bowie knife at his belt, and handed the shotgun to his brother. Protection to them meant bear traps or a twelve-gauge, and they didn't see those either.

"What is, Preacher?" Deeter asked.

"The songs. Woven into the notes are charms and spells of celestial love. A granny witch has composed this, and they play it well under her direction."

"Sure is a catchy tune, right 'nuff."

Duffy still had Mrs. Hoopkins's cutting knife in his belt and he slid the handle aside for an easy draw. He said, "Some nice ladies' voices carryin' it just fine too, reelin' right along with the washboard. About time we stopped off for some companionship with the feminine persuadin'. I'm'a feelin' a might lonely after all this travelin'."

"And I smell hog cracklins!"

"They got themselves a right proper hootenanny goin' on. I say we get out of this rain and have us a terrible ruckus of fun."

The archangels pressed their hands to Jester's face. Like over-eager children they flew and returned with more and more images and knowledge that he couldn't fully understand. He dropped his chin to his chest as the shadows roamed about him, within and without, fluttering their great wings and confiding their tender testimonies, urging him onward. His life and death had been a trial before the eyes of man and God, and it still wasn't over. Would never be over. He needed the daughter that should have been his. He needed the grandchild that would share his burden. He deserved the family that had been denied him before.

He said, "It grows dark. Wait until the moon rises and then we'll visit ourselves upon our swamp neighbors. Until then, leave me."

"Leave you?" Deeter asked. "Just where in the hell we gonna go, preacher?"

Jester turned and his eyes pulsed with energy. Duffy tugged at his brother's arm and drew him back through the palm leaves. "Let's just let the preacher go on about his own business. We'll go sit down the creek this'a way."

"Well then, I'm in agreement," Deeter said, "let's get on. But I'm a'gonna get some hog cracklins 'fore this night is through."

As they moved off, the ghost of Jester's murdered wife—*the wife he had murdered*—appeared beside him and said, "You claim you've done this for family, but you destroyed the one you had. If-fun you cared so much about kith and kin, you'd not have been so anxious with the blade."

The voice again, and always, so much more than her own, filled with the kind of peace he craved and could not contain.

"It's no empty claim," Jester said. "I've a right to my own fulfillment and serenity."

She stroked the bone-white curls at his neck, the way she would during summer picnics at the river, after the baptisms. "By warming your hands in the blood of children?"

"I've never hurt a child yet."

"Oh," she said, as if stricken. "You forget."

And it was true, he suddenly realized, he had forgotten. The child rushing him, the hatchet, the struggle. Here he was following the trail of his true enemy, and he had ignored how close they'd once been, even at his bleakest hour.

Brother Jester said, "My mistakes were made for love. Anything done for love is beyond the righteous and the wrathful."

"That's an excuse meant to soothe your scratched heart."

"God's will is greater than man's."

"You speak with such conviction on judgments left best to the Lord," his dead wife said.

"I speak with the tongue He gave me. It's what I've always done. Back when I had a honeyed voice and now that I don't. I've always spoken the words He presents me."

Her ghost, despite knowing the harmony of the afterworld, looked almost aggrieved for a moment.

"You'll not see me at your side again," she said. "Does that worry you?"

"Yes."

"Take my hand and let your pain end."

"There was a reason I murdered you," he said. "And I have not forgotten or forgiven it."

"If only you'd ever loved as well as you learned to hate, these last twenty years wouldn't have been so empty."

"Better than being dead."

"You are dead," she reminded him.

"I'll miss you," Jester said, his ruined voice thick with emotion, and in turning he knew he would no longer find her there.

And then seeing he was alone he understood he truly had nothing now, and the child seemed that much more important.

He remembered the all-night sings during the tent gatherings and revivals, when he'd stand in a pulpit surrounded by the lame and the blind and the abandoned and the damned and the doomed, and side by side with a golden-voiced boy he'd feel the will of God flowing through his hands and he would heal them all.

They would praise the name of Jesus and kiss Jester's palms and hug the boy, and the evils of the world would perish for a moment, an hour, a night. He'd end his summers staring up at the stars and listening to the evening gales rolling in, and the sweetness of life would fill him until he wept. While at home in his bed his wife had taken up with Bliss Nail, and the arrival of his own oblivion fell upon him.

Now he was back, and the shielding music played, and the golden-voiced boy was now a man who awaited him. Another circle was about to close. Jester stood and moved toward the creek. He was ready.

Despite the storm clouds, the stars began to shine down. Jester smiled, crossed his arms, and hugged himself as he walked, and the sweetness of life filled him once more so full of love that he wept black flame for what would soon be his.

 # Chapter 21

Duffy and Deeter danced with two women older than their ma—older than their ma would've been if they hadn't ushered her off with the ax handle—while the jug and washboard band continued to play up on a porch and the drizzle came down.

The sun had set but the swamp folk had party lights strung up along a couple of porches and down the main street. Duffy had found himself a bottle half full of corn liquor and Deeter had hog cracklins falling from his mouth while they swung arm in arm with the ladies.

The women, though a little older than the Ferris boys generally liked, were still firm and fleshy and had most of their teeth, so the brothers didn't mind much. The fact that one of the ladies seemed to have an extra eye staring out from beneath the ringlets of her hair, and the other was such a fine dancer because she had three legs to leap around upon, initially gave the Ferris boys some pause.

But they figured what the hell and hopped to it anyway, since they were hungry for food and company, and they figured to have some regular good old fun before they got to the killing.

The women had already gone soft on Deeter and Duffy, the way most ladies did. Duffy tried not to let the third eye throw off his two-step, even though it sort of kept peering at him in a somewhat suspicious manner. Deeter was having fun trying to keep up with the three-legged gal who was more or less running circles around him.

"You boys sure do know how to kick up a good time," the three-legged gal said.

"Nowhere near as good as you, honey!" Deeter squawked out, laughing. He threw his arms around her and hugged her to him, thinking this would be a good bundle of woman to go to bed with each night and wake up beside every morning. He was in a marrying mood.

The Ferris boys hadn't been to a good old-fashioned hootenanny since at least last summer, or maybe even the summer before, although with all the moonshine often being poured among their friends and neighbors along the way, it was hard to recall the specifics. A good jug and washboard band was a rarity in Enigma. A fine banjo-player even more so. Working the mash vats didn't leave a man with much wind left and hardly no skin on his fingertips.

"Darlin'," Duffy said to the three-eyed woman, "what do you see with that extra one right there?"

"I sometimes glimpse the future," she said, staring directly at him. And when this gal stared directly at you, she well and truly *stared*.

"That right? Well, then you tell me this. Are you gazin' on anything of great or minor import at this here very moment?"

"I am."

"And what is it?" Duffy asked, eyeballing the eyeball that eyeballed him. The girl's wet hair closed over it and he reached up and parted her ringlets. "You got me curious."

"I see you being chased by gators."

The eye blinked at him, and shifted in her head to look him up and down.

"I don't get chased, darlin', I do the chasin'. I killed me more than twenty bulls in the last month."

"You're a poacher then." She smiled and her two normal eyes seemed almost adoring, and the third one looked like it was sneering at him.

"We're just businessmen, me and my brother," Duffy said, wondering if he punched the extra eye would the girl take offense. Maybe she'd tell him, Hit it again, I never did like that little glaring bastard.

"You're screaming," she said. "You're croaking."

"I'm what?"

"Croaking like they do. Making those awful noises."

He tried to continue grinning but this gal was wearing on his good mood. He checked Deeter and was surprised at how much fun his brother was having, just swinging and swaying about, eating his hog cracklins and tapping at some moon. "So you're sayin' they catch me, these gators?"

"Looked mighty close," the three-eyed woman said. "I just flashed on it for a moment."

For some reason that got him laughing, and even though the eyeball was definitely glowering now, wishing him hurt, the music swelled around Duffy and some of the brutal thoughts that had started to go through his head, like how he might want to jam Mrs. Hoopkins's cutting knife right into this gal's third peeper, began to fade. He hugged her again and she tittered in his ear, and that was just fine.

Beside him, Deeter wasn't dancing so much as he was rushing around in a circle trying to get his hands on the tri-legged gal who was really moving at a near-gallop. Duffy reached out and caught the jug of moonshine and took a hefty swallow.

Abruptly, Deeter stopped dancing and let his partner go, gripped Duffy by the arm, and pulled him aside out of the party lights and beneath a palmetto where he'd stood the shotgun.

"Lookie there!" Deeter said.

"What?"

"It's the big red fella walkin' down this mud track toward us."

Duffy frowned and took another swig. "He's Jester's worry, none'a ours."

"'Less he spotted our faces when we tried to run him over.'"

"It was too dark out, but just to make sure, let's go sit inside for a while with the others, have us some more food and get another jug."

"I like that idea, but what if Jester gets irate that we ain't on the job?"

"We still don't know what the job is except Jester needs him somebody to keep him from sailing off into the sky when that black evil is upon him."

"I do wish he never stumbled onto us," Deeter said.

"Well, who knows how this will turn out? There may be somethin' to gain here before it's all over. I recognize some of these swamp folk from Enigma. They come into town for their pension checks and supplies. And they ain't got no sheriff out here, no sir. Seems to me we could walk through this town and take just about anythin' we might want, and if anybody speaks up about it, with one mouth or possibly two or more, well, I figure that might be the last thing they ever do say on this green earth."

Deeter smiled and said, "They got some catfish and taters set out on the table. Let's go get us a dish, and then we'll go a'visitin'. Ask around about Jester's girl that he wants so bad, just to keep on the safe side of his ill will."

"Good idea."

As thunder snarled overhead, they stepped up into the house where the folk milled about, grabbing food and drink and whooping with laughter. The Ferris boys had catfish with sugar beets, and wandered about the large living room looking at the various freakish natures of some of these people.

There went a dwarf with two huge feet who bounced along doing his best not to get stomped on or tripped over. And here came a squirming worm gal who inched along like a caterpillar, which tickled Deeter's imagination in ways it had never been excited before. And in the corner stood two young boys—no, just one young'un who had nearly two complete faces right there stuck on his head, one mouth chewing and the other swallowing down a cup of goat's milk. It did fire the mind, thinking about what these folk were all about here in the deep swamp, and what their days and nights must be like.

Over the years the Ferris boys had done a bit of work for industries near and far, helping bring in chemicals and waste, showing the northerners what the safest places were to dump. Now, as they each finished up a plate of catfish, they wondered if they shouldn't have held off on eating as much as they had, considering the state of the local waters and dirt. Then they shrugged and ate a bit more and grabbed hold of the nearest jug, which wasn't moon but a sweet warm cider.

Eventually a couple of the band members decided on a break and two others took over their instruments, continuing on with the music. Even a hootenanny usually had a quiet moment or two, but these folk, they just didn't know how to settle down it seemed.

The banjo player came inside to have a plate of greens and a tap of dandelion wine. The man who replaced him on the porch wasn't nearly as talented, plucking at the strings like he was scratching a tomcat. The song didn't sail anymore, didn't really move into the center of you the way it had before.

Deeter felt an odd twist at the back of his head and approached the musician sipping his wine. "You sure can play that banjo," he said. "Our daddy knew a chord or two, but he needed to have a few taps of moon 'fore he could play worth a damn. A'course, a few taps too many and he couldn't hardly find the strings no more and he'd come chase us with the rake."

The banjo strummer blinked a couple of times, sizing Deeter up, keeping his lips peeled back and his teeth on show. "Why, ah, thank you for them kind words, son, I surely do appreciate them."

"That new boy out there can't hardly bend a string without it screaming."

"He's new to the village and fancies himself a self-taught geetar player. He figures if a banjo looks near the same then it ought to play near the same."

"Figures wrong there, eh?"

"Sure does, but he was a botherin' me to play, and I wanted myself a plate of greens, so we're both happy." The musician swallowed back more wine, looked at his heaped plate, and said, "Well now, you give your daddy my best. Maybe he and I can strum a song or two together someday."

"Naw, he's dead," Deeter told him. "Long while gone now."

"Well, that's a damn shame, I'm sorry as hell to hear that there."

"Don't be, he was a mean son of a bitch, and he deserved twice what he got, but I was only a young'un and couldn't hardly swing the ax handle all that well. Though it was fun shootin' his toe off."

"Pardon?"

Deeter grinned and said, "We're lookin' for Sarah."

"Sarah who?"

Duffy, who'd been watching the big red fella through the window, stepped closer and said, "Sarah the pregnant girl who come through here last night with two other pregnant girls after they landed in a skiff, I'm'a thinkin'. That Sarah. You recall her now?"

"No."

"You are one contrary cuss, now ain't you?" Deeter said.

"No, I just ain't seen no pregnant girl come through, much less three of them."

"I think you must be lyin'."

"And what right do you have to say that to me?"

"This," Deeter told him, yanking his Bowie knife from its sheathe and plunging it into the banjo player's throat.

Duffy said, "Well, we're back in it now," and stuck a hand out. He grabbed hold of the three-eyed gal as she came through the door and drew her close, kissing her hard on the lips while she tried to yell.

"Looks like the picnic's over, folks," Deeter said as the rest of the folk screamed and cried out, and the catfish hit the floor, "and the ruckus is about to start." He reached over to grab the last bag of hog cracklins but some fat old boy wouldn't let them go, so taken with the sight of the dead banjo player he was. Deeter picked up the shotgun and blasted the chubby coot through the gizzard, and then the Ferris boys stepped outside into the cool rain and leaned against the porch railing wondering which girl to go after now.

Like Brother Jester had said, at least they were good for murder.

CHAPTER 22

Hellboy heard the shouts and shrieking and ran up to the house where the band had been playing. People poured out into the road. The party lights gave off a sickly blue, red, and green cast in the swamp. The moon crawled out from cover and then slid back in.

Up on the veranda, two yahoos were terrorizing a woman who looked like she had a third eye in the middle of her forehead. A fiddle player had been caught in the corner and couldn't decide whether he should run and jump the rail or just stand there cowering. A woman with no limbs inchwormed along down the stairs and Hellboy gestured for the fiddler to follow. He clutched his bow to his chest and ran.

Hellboy got up on the first step and saw the dead man lying on the floor inside, blood still bubbling from his mouth. And beside him was another catfish.

Always back to the catfish.

There wasn't any cool way to say it, so he just let it rip. "Okay, you two creeps, let the girl go."

It sounded even dumber than he'd been expecting.

One of the mooks waved a shotgun around without really pointing it and said, "Hellfire, son, I s'pect your mama drank herself more than a jug of poisoned moon in her time."

The other said, "And ate herself too much fried goat, I'm thinkin'. Now, you git on away from us, big fella."

"So let me guess. You're the Ferris brothers?"

"That's right, I'm Deeter and this is Duffy, and we're lookin' for Sarah."

"Why?" Hellboy asked.

That stopped the brothers. They looked at each other unsure of how to answer. They still didn't quite understand what the hell Jester wanted with her.

So Deeter just said, "That ain't none'a your concern now, friend. You get on with your evenin' and we'll get on with ours. Yours is waitin' for you down the creek."

Hellboy glanced at the water rolling onward. "That where this Jester is?"

"He most sure and truly is, and he's talkin' to God or the dead or maybe he's floatin' two three feet offa the ground, but he surely is waitin' on you."

"Terrific."

Nodding, Hellboy figured one good punch and he could bring half the porch roof down on these two mooks, but he was afraid the girl might be hurt in the process. He couldn't leave her to them, and finesse wasn't exactly his strong suit. He had to keep these two talking and was about to ask another question, find out what this Jester was really all about, when the woman smiled at him and shook her head.

"You don't have to worry about me," she said. "They won't hurt me or anyone else."

Duffy said, "Darlin', much as I like gazin' into them three limpid pools of yours, you givin' this good ole boy here some bad advice all around."

The woman stared at Hellboy, ignoring the Ferris brothers. "Trust me, I've had a prophetic flash and already seen how this is going to end. That's my gift. Leave them to me for the time being. You've got your own trial awaiting you."

"I think that's enough out of you," Duffy said, and got out Mrs. Hoopkins's cutting knife and tapped her on the cheek with it. "Say no more or your bloodlettin' begins."

"You're going to croak and scream."

"You done tole me that already tonight. I just gotta say, this was one fine hootenanny until you had to go and spoil it with all that strange talk. Can't a good ole boy just kick up his heels and have himself a plate of greens without so much bother?"

Hellboy had met precognitives before, and she had the same sense of calm that the others had, who had learned to accept the inevitable. On a couple of different occasions, in Brazil and the Himalayas, he'd tried to change the course of events and soon found that he'd played into the hand of fate, directly bringing about what he'd been trying to alter.

It still went against his gut, doing nothing, but he'd gleaned a thing or two about believing in others who might know more than he did.

He nodded to her and she nodded back and said, "Your true heart is your strength, remember that."

"Sure," he told her and turned toward the green darkness.

"You see yourself drawin' your own last breath?" Duffy asked the three-eyed lady, genuinely curious. "'Cause I'm a figuring that ain't much of a gift, knowing your own ending. Which way you get it, in the chest?" Tapping her over the heart with the cutting blade. "Or the belly?" Moving the knife down her chest to her stomach. The excitement lit his eyes.

"Neither."

"I was always partial to the neck," Deeter put in. "Plenty of gushin' but it's over early, and if you sidestep quick enough you don't get nothin' on your clothes. Oh, and don't forget to ask her where this Sarah is."

"That's right," Duffy said, now that he'd been reminded. "Where's this pregnant girl Sarah? Your extra peeper see where she's currently at?"

"As a matter of fact, it does."

"Where then?"

"I won't tell you."

"You don't tell me then you gonna die screamin' and croakin'." Duffy let out a laugh at that, feeling glad that he'd finally had the chance to turn around some of that spooky talk she'd been giving him.

"I'll take you to her," the three-eyed woman said, gazing deeply at the beautiful Ferris boys, and then far beyond them.

"Stay close to the woods," Deeter said. "I hear lots of whisperin' out there. We run into anyone, and we gonna let loose a lot more blood."

Hellboy wandered down the creek and got turned around in the dark. The water ran on his right but, somehow, after he moved around a loblolly bush and got caught in some briar, the creek was suddenly on his left, or at least sounded like it.

He turned and saw the lights of town still burning behind him. He hoped this wasn't another game like with Granny Lewt's shack just moving around and the swamp coming with her. He wondered if the best course of action wouldn't be to start calling for Jester and see if the guy actually answered.

Sometimes you just wanted to ask some troublemaker, Exactly what the hell is your problem, buddy?

Stray flickers of lightning lit the far-off skies. Above, the moon continued to claw through the clouds. Hellboy smelled the fragrance of night-blooming flowers. He raised his stone fist and wondered what Jester's shadows had discovered about him, through his own dreams.

Did they know things he didn't know himself? The rain covered his hand and dripped off. He called into the night, "All right already! Come on, let's get to it!"

Only silence except for the slap of the creek and the bull gators roaring in the distance.

When there was no response he wheeled back through the thistles, found out exactly where the creek was, and eventually made his way back to the village. Maybe it was a setup and he'd been lured away on purpose. He moved fast, shouldering aside the brush, keeping his eye on those colorful lights.

Oddly enough, he didn't feel lost or even particularly anxious. Perhaps he'd picked up on some of that prescient tranquility. Even Lament appeared to have a touch of it, all this acceptance and belief in the big Kahuna.

Enough was enough. Hellboy picked up his pace and made it back to the main street of the village. He started walking up it like Wyatt Earp doing his thing. No one else was about. They were hiding in their houses, waiting for resolution. He didn't blame them for inaction. The most tranquil places were the ones always thrown into misery when strangers stepped in. They'd welcomed, fed, and tended to him. Now it was time for payback.

Hellboy stopped and listened for the sound of children but heard nothing. He called out to Jester again, "You're slick with shadows, even hiding in them. How about you step out and we get on with this thing?"

Sometimes it worked.

From down the road appeared a figure in a frock coat, who started forward toward Hellboy. He even had a black hat on. Hellboy watched this old guy coming at him, so gaunt that he looked like a strong breeze would carry him sailing away. But you couldn't judge troublemakers by their size. Some of the worst he'd ever tangled with had barely reached his knee.

He could tell right off there was something about Brother Jester you couldn't take lightly. It was there all about him, even in the darkness—the writhing shadows that contorted in greater blackness.

Jester walked down the dirt track between shanties and smiled the only smile he probably knew. The one that spoke of death.

"I know your secret heart," the dark preacher said in his blight-ed voice.

"Now that would be a *really* neat trick," Hellboy told him.

"You believe so?"

"Yeah, 'cause I don't even know it. I go out of my way not to know it. That's how I manage to get up in the morning."

"I'll show you then. It is my gift to you."

He reached into his pocket and then withdrew his hand, which he held out to Hellboy.

It was empty.

Not exactly the showiest gimmick Hellboy had ever seen, but he figured more was coming, and it was bound to be bad. So he said, "Screw this," and hauled off to give Brother Jester a good smack in the chops.

The mad preacher caught Hellboy's wrist in his own thin, frail hand, and stopped it cold. He brushed over the knuckles gently with his fingers, almost lovingly, the same way that piece of shadow had.

"Hey now," Hellboy said, "that's just not possible—" and watched as Brother Jester's own pale fist began to turn red and grow thicker and change into a great stone hand of doom.

In seconds it was no different from Hellboy's fist, which Jester drew back with a crazed leer, his teeth turning black and crack-ling with energy as he began to laugh, and then punched Hellboy through the nearest shack.

It hurt like hell.

 CHAPTER 23

Shadows rose from Brother Jester and slid forward, racing around Hellboy, veiling him, and entering him.

This was a different kind of darkness. It was his nightmare come alive. He felt his own history being drawn up from him and dispersed. His memories, his hurts, his knowledge, anger, the lessons learned, his love, even the confusion. And everything else that made him what he was.

He struggled to grab the forbidding wraiths, feeling them beat and flap against his chest like wings. But they were insubstantial, ethereal, and he couldn't grab hold despite what they bled from him.

Luckily the shanty was empty. He was on his back in a child's bed. The frame, made from cut logs and lashed together with twine, had been crushed to kindling beneath his weight. A smiling rag doll with pearl-button eyes had flopped off a shelf into his face. On the floor lay a smashed chalkboard slate covered with a kid's drawings. A Hellboy-sized hole had been torn through the front wall.

He reached for the shadows again and said, "Hold it, you're not taking any pieces of me away with you—"

They slid across the floor and ceiling, the grand forms of archangels turning their faces toward him, nodding, their lips moving to speak words he couldn't hear. Divinity taking a cheap shot at you for no reason you could name. Didn't everybody already have to put up with that enough?

When the shadows receded back to Jester, who stood just outside the hole in the wall, the preacher almost seemed frightened for a moment before he began to laugh. Hellboy clambered out of the kid's busted bed thinking how awful it could have been. A child dead by his own hand. He clenched his teeth and climbed out of the wreckage.

"Let's try that again," Hellboy said, rushing from the shack and swinging his fist once more at the dark preacher.

Jester caught him by the throat in one superhumanly quick movement, then yanked Hellboy off his feet until they were nose to nose. The boiling motes of energy leaking from Jester's eyes burned into Hellboy's brain. Blood leaked from his nose and mouth. Hellboy clubbed at Jester but he couldn't move the emaciated codger an inch. Not only was he in trouble, but considering Jester weighed about eighty-two pounds, this situation was damn degrading. About the best he could do was knock the hat off. It didn't make him feel any better.

"We are both similar creatures, you and I," Jester said.

Hellboy gasped, "Now you're just . . . being . . . mean."

"We were set on our courses long before our births, game pieces of God. Slaves to Heaven and Hell."

"Go take . . . a flying jump, pal."

"We have walked both paths, the left and the right. We're closer than you think. Almost brothers."

Fighting the pain, swallowing back screams, Hellboy tried to kick out, but he couldn't get any purchase with his hooves.

The mad preacher said, "You are full of sin and that sin gives me strength."

"Screw you, you son of a—"

The whispering shadows swarmed over Hellboy until they covered him completely, within and without, as he stood in the dim moonlight with shimmers of lightning cracking the heavens. He felt the feathered darkness prying into every crevice of his mind and soul, sweeping back through his life. Reveling in certain memories, almost soothing him during others, and finding his most unbearable moments and pitying him for them. He set his lips and blood ran down his chin and flicked among the winged shades. He could almost see eyes there, peering at him forlornly.

Hellboy tried to raise himself against them, and tore again at Jester's hand on his throat. The frail white fingers dug in with even more furious strength. It would've been funny if he wasn't being throttled.

He kicked out, planted his hooves on Jester's chest, and finally managed to fling himself away. He landed hard, rolling in the mud, hacking and sucking air. He stood and turned, ready for the next attack.

Except there wasn't one.

Brother Jester's arms were thrown open, his head forced back. His mouth grew wide and flaming motes of arcane power drifted from his lips and nostrils. Something nasty was happening but Jester appeared happy about it. He climbed into the air, inch by inch.

Hellboy watched and shook his head and sighed. He had no idea what was happening but it couldn't be good. Jester laughed although he was clearly in agony, one of those penitents who can do incredible feats because their faith carried them through.

Ma'am McCulver said Jester had performed miracles and brought God to the swamp. So what did this guy believe in now?

"You want to tell me why you're so interested in this one pregnant girl?" Hellboy shouted at the levitating form. "Just because Bliss Nail and your wife played hanky panky once upon a time? You really think that's worth all this grief you've been causing for twenty years? You know she's not your daughter. You know we can't let you take her baby. You're acting like an idiot."

Jester came down fast, still laughing, but his eyes were pinwheeling. Good, it meant the guy had his weak spot.

"You've no right to judge me, demon. Your secret heart is so much worse than mine."

"Thought you were going to show it to me."

"I have."

"So far I just see a trickster playing games."

"You're blind to yourself. Which is how you wish it to be. But I'll give you the boon of sight."

For some reason Hellboy didn't like the sound of that. The shadows reared and swarmed forward again, like a crowd of helpful people moving to lend a hand, who only wind up suffocating the person they're trying to help. He could feel them now, within him again, and he realized they weren't evil and weren't truly a part of Jester.

Hellboy sensed they were as immature, unknowing, naive, adventuresome, and curious as the swamp kids.

He realized then that the crying children he'd been hearing for two days were these angels. Perhaps the lost offspring of God. Or perhaps the lost scion of mankind.

He looked at the preacher and said, "Okay, playtime's over, pal."

"This has never been a game or joy. It's duty and blessing."

Jester stood over him now, his forehead bulging with nubby horns. They grew larger and curved and jutted higher. The old man's face grew broad and flat. His rail-thin body thickened and turned red until Hellboy faced another version himself, damn near exactly the same except for the eyes.

"I know your true nature."

"You don't know squat about me, pal."

He reached out and grabbed Jester's horns, the ones that had grown merely to taunt him, he figured. As he'd done with his own, he snapped them off and held them like curved blades, feeling the damnation and power they represented. He hated to admit it but this was a good feeling, a familiar one. He thrust them through Jester's heart.

"Suck on that, buddy!" he shouted.

But nothing happened.

"We are destroyers," the dark preacher said, "and we are the destroyed."

The stone fist swung out again.

And all Hellboy had time to say was, "Oh crap."

Then he couldn't say or think of anything because his mind and body were composed of nothing but agony. He hurtled high into the cypresses, and the land where Jester had brought God sailed away far beneath him.

The shadow children, the great seraphim, cried and crooned.

Clinging to the dark brush, with Duffy's hand squeezing her arm roughly, the three-eyed girl pointed to Ma'am McCulver's house and said, "There. The girl you want is inside. She's just had a baby."

"What's that place?" Duffy asked.

"It's the granny witch's home."

"You people and all your hag houses."

"Looks like Jester's a granddaddy," Deeter said. He held up the shotgun, looking for trouble, but didn't see anybody. "This young'un got himself an extra leg or nose or ear? He got a chin on his forehead? He got a red tail?"

"It's a baby girl," the three-eyed woman told him, "and no, she's what the world calls normal."

"What I'd call normal then too, honeypie."

"You're a cruel malignancy." The woman turned away, as if unable to witness the awful sight of the beautiful Ferris boys. "You'll die tonight with your brother."

"Yeah, how so?"

"By your own misdeeds. By the hand of your master."

"Ain't got no master, missy," Deeter told her. "I'm my own man, and don't you forget it none 'lest I carve out your liver for you."

"Aw, forget her ranting," Duffy said. "She does go on and on, just like Ma if you recall."

"I do recollect."

"This one here, she got the brain damage, I s'pect, from that third eye growing out her head. It affects the noggin."

"Don't see how it couldn't."

The door to Ma'am McCulver's home, the witchy palace, opened and out came Doc Wayburn, who trundled off across town muttering to himself.

A minute later, out came John Lament, not so full of his usual vim but still looking strong and a touch larger than he should. The Ferris boys ducked down and dragged the girl with them, watching through the brush. In the moonlight Lament's white streak burned bright, and so did his eyes, filled with—well, the Ferris brothers couldn't quite tell what they were filled with. Whether it was joy or fear or a combination of both. Duffy and Deeter had run afoul of John Lament plenty of times over the years, and mostly they wound up with bleeding heads, cracked bones, and bruised egos. They'd been wanting to kill him for a month of blue Sundays, but it never seemed the right time.

"Should I put two shells in his back?" Deeter asked.

"I don't like his look of conviction. Let Jester handle him too. Makes our night a little less complicated. We're just here to get the girl and hand her over. Then we steal what we can pocket and get the hell back to Enigma, free of that crazy preacher."

"No need to play coy," Deeter said. "Iffun that granny wants trouble we'll give it to her. Otherwise, we march up and kick in the door, take the girl, and we're off."

Thanks to the rain the town was brimming with puddles. They started toward the house but before they'd gotten to the porch, the door opened. Sarah stepped out holding her newborn daughter wrapped in a yellow Easter blanket.

Behind her came Ma'am McCulver and the pumpkin-headed boy who glowered and tried to look mean but just couldn't do much. Especially considering his little tuft of hair was swaying so humorously back and forth in the breeze. The boy moved out in front and met the Ferris brothers at the foot of the steps.

"What you want, jughead?" Duffy asked.

The pumpkin-headed boy hauled off and socked Duffy in the face. It was the first punch he'd ever thrown, and he seemed sad and stupefied to have thrown it at all, but at least Duffy let go of the three-eyed woman. Or at least he did so after Fishboy Lenny swam out from a mud puddle and sank his teeth back into Duffy's ankle.

Duffy yowled, looked down, and saw the godamnedest sight he'd ever seen. There was a kid down there gnawing on his foot, flapping his flipper hands around and keeping afloat in the puddle. Duffy started dancing around but the boy just looked up and his mouth was red in the porch light and his needle-sharp tiny teeth were strung with bits of Duffy's flesh.

Deeter shouted, "Hellfire!" He aimed the ten-gauge but couldn't draw a bead with all the sudden activity. The pumpkin-headed kid dove for him, grabbed the barrel of the shotgun, and tried to grapple it loose. Deeter held onto the stock with one hand and pummeled the boy to his knees with the other.

The weirdo fish kid went, "Fweep."

"This ain't no gator, girl!"

"No," the three-eyed woman said, "that's Lenny."

"Fweep mwash," went Fishboy Lenny.

"He done chewed up my foot!"

Deeter said, "I'm gonna have to shotgun him into next Sunday now. Seen that before, did you?"

"No, it was new to me."

"Reckon you need a fourth eye for that, huh?"

"Enough," Ma'am McCulver said, stepping into the moonlight, the pale silver illumination embracing and enhancing her beauty. Her presence was both calming and fearsome. Her black hair was a mass of wild curls that rose and reached. Fishboy Lenny tugged at the nearly unconscious pumpkin-headed boy and drew him away through the mud.

Ma'am McCulver scowled, and the wind grew louder and the storm suddenly seemed closer. The Ferris brothers didn't know what to make of any of this witchy business and simply stood there, wondering who to kill next.

Sarah said, "Please, Ma'am, this is a family argument. It's my fight and no one else's. Only I can do anythin' about it and put a stop to all the fuss."

"I know you," Duffy said to Sarah, "least I almost reckon I do. We seen you about."

"You have," she told them.

Deeter said, "You're Sarah, the girl been causin' us so much trouble."

"Deeter Ferris," she said, "you're one rotten soul, through and through. And how is it I've caused you any bother?"

"Well, the bother really started a bit before you was even mentioned, when we were takin' care of the lady saleswoman in the swamp, but anyways a bother you've become all right, thanks to Jester."

Duffy released the three-eyed woman and grabbed Sarah's arm instead. Her sleeping baby sighed loudly. He held his cutting blade to Sarah's cheek, turned to Ma'am McCulver and said, "Now that's it, no more trouble! You gonna raise a hand to me, you gorgeous piece of love?"

"I won't. It will do no good."

"Glad you reckon that. You gonna keep that jughead and fish-head away from us?"

She held out her arm and the pumpkin-headed boy climbed to his feet, stepped close to her, and laid the side of his bleeding face against her chest. Fishboy Lenny swam up and rested against her knee.

"All apostles must face their masters on their own," Ma'am McCulver said. "You two evil brothers are no different."

Deeter stared at the granny witch and a crazed leer split his face. "I'll be back for you, darlin', and we'll have ourselves a good he couldn't save. Nearly all the dead seemed to know about such things now, chatting him up around the water coolers of the abyss.

"Shut up," he said as he walked by.

"What's that?" the houseman asked.

"Nothing, Jeeves."

The houseman spun. A pretty dramatic move for an old guy like that. "My name's Waldridge. I been takin' care'a the Nail family since I was still a child of twelve. Same as my daddy and his daddy before him. You might frown on my life, find it worth snickering about—"

"Hey now, wait a minute, buddy—"

"—but I don't let no man, whether he's white or black or red, speak to me with contempt. I don't care how big you are, suh, I promise to knock you down iffun you call me Jeeves again."

"Okay, Waldridge," Hellboy said, "you've straightened me out. Now lead on."

The paintings kept up their chatter but beneath it Hellboy thought he could hear something else. He cocked his head, focusing, and there it was again. The sound of an infant crying.

Withdrawing an Agnus Dei candle from his gris-gris pouch, Hellboy saw the wick immediately sputter and spark to life. He pinched the flame out. The old man in the truck had been right. A lot of black luck ran wild in this house. But that didn't mean much in itself. If enough blood ran inside a place there were usually enough echoes of regret, grief, and pain to call ancient forces and all manner of brazen, gluttonous things out of the mud.

Waldridge crept along the hall, opening huge double doors and then closing them again, the mansion as frayed but clean as the man himself. Ten coats of paint couldn't cover the hard years seaming the walls and floors. The original oil lamps were now friezes, the curtains heavy with lost heritage. They passed a ballroom lined with antlered animal heads.

Hellboy replaced the agnus dei and opened the small compartment on his belt that held a charm he'd received at the Dome of

# CHAPTER 4

People had been dying out here by the dozens since the beginning of the world, swallowed by the bayou without a ripple. Or found hanging in the cypresses after a week of being lost in the maze of green, tormented by swimming snakes, alligators, and half-pound spiders.

Tourists came for the gator farms, tent revivals, hootenannies, and jamborees. Hellboy still didn't know what he'd come for, but he was glad he had a reason now to do the only thing he knew how to do.

As he walked the empty road he sensed the scrub around him beginning to encroach, the night growing heavier and blacker, reaching for him. He stopped, stood still, and watched as the tree branches whirled and clawed past the moon. The ground shifted, alive, advancing and somehow taking him along with it. In the distance ahead he watched as . . . as *the distance itself* came closer without real movement. The road began to flood, abruptly filling not only with rising water but with cypress, titi, and hard-packed earth. The marsh prairie came alive and rushed forward to meet and surround him.

Before him now stood a small one-room shack.

"Now that was a pretty neat trick," he said. Stepping over, he waited for someone to come out. No one did.

Hellboy thought, All of that and they're going to make me knock.

ole time, I promise. We'll have us some catfish and pumpkin pie for snackin'."

"You'll be dead within the hour," the three-eyed girl said.

Deeter looked back at his brother and said, "For swamp folk who know how to kick up a fine hootenanny, these people are startin' to work on my nerves some!"

"Mine too," Duffy said. "We'll burn the whole place down before we leave." He looked at Sarah and told her, "Come on along, little miss. Your daddy is waitin' on you."

 CHAPTER 24

You are many things, the children said, *bonded of great love and extreme hatred. Power and resilience. Ego and narrowminded bias. Threatened and threat. Hopeful and hope. He is remote and He is not. He is vast and He is not. He is here within you and He is not. You are. You are in need of acknowledgment and response. Your questions can never be answered because He is beyond understanding. You rely on faith. This is the distance between you and Him, you and the Almighty. We seek to bring the world closer. We seek to reopen Eden. We dream of taking down the flaming swords at the gates of the garden. It is our duty and our grace. We are mistaken, we have much to learn. We give thanks for your efforts. We love. He loves. You love.* The children wailed because it was what children do. Because they couldn't understand all they were and all that was around them in the great divine experiment of humanity. They were lost, in need of their father.

Hellboy came down like a sputtering V-2 rocket and crashed through another shanty.

This one wasn't empty. This one had a family in it. A pretty large family packed into a tiny place. A man and a woman, two children, an elderly lady, and an old dude in a rattan wheelchair. Everybody was huddled to one side of the shack holding on to each other. The roof was mostly gone. The little girl was wide-eyed and on the verge of tears. Hellboy's head was on fire.

He'd landed in the fireplace and the flames lashed at him. The precocious shadows weighed on top of him, still inquisitive, nosy even, tickling the underside of his mind. They were trying desperately to communicate, drilling into his brain.

It wasn't easy, just letting this kind of thing go on, kids making mudpies in your memories, but he decided not to fight them this time.

He let them take whatever pieces from him they wanted. Whatever memories they needed to sift, drawing up his experiences and holding them before their own interest and attention.

Maybe Jester was right and they were similar creatures. Hellboy thought about being the destroyed and the destroyer. It was the truth that always lay within him that he refused to acknowledge. It was how he lived. He never dealt with what he was. He never thought about it and just did what he was supposed to do.

He didn't know the shadow children, but they knew him.

"Ain't your head hurt?" the old lady asked. She bent and peered at him. "Pull it outta the fire. Ain't you got no sense?"

Hellboy sat up. "Ouch."

"You ain't burned much. I got some salve if you need it." Then she grunted and sucked at her gums. "Well, I did have some. Looks like you done mashed it beyond use."

"Sorry."

"Mama," the little boy said, "it's the devil."

"It ain't the devil, son."

"It looks like the devil. His skin is red."

"He just been out in the sun too long, and stickin' his head in the fire. You hush now, son."

The girl stared at him, trying not to cry. He wanted to console her. He had no idea how.

Clambering up, he stood and looked around the shack. He'd seen a few miracles in his time and thought this might be one for the books. The room was maybe ten by ten. Six people in it.

Hellboy had missed them all. What were the chances?

He said, "Sorry about the mess."

"A mess is what you make when you spill the porridge," the old man said, rolling forward. He couldn't get far because there was too much smashed lumber about. "This is a whole other matter now."

"Sorry about the whole other matter."

"It don't mean nothin', we'll fix it and get on by. What's of greater pertinence is you gettin' out there and kickin' them nasty fellas outta our village."

"You're right. Consider it done."

"I'll consider it done after you finish doin' it."

Hellboy marched out the door, tasting blood and glancing once more at the family behind, the children scared but both slightly grinning, the old woman nodding to him once.

When he turned to look outside once more, Brother Jester was stroking black flames from his chin, and Lament was there playing his mouth-harp.

Lament stood facing Brother Jester beneath the brightening moonlight, neither of them looking particularly upset or angry. In fact, they appeared rather relaxed. Like two old friends at odds for the moment, after a bitter but brief quarrel, who knew they'd make up soon. Lament kept plucking away, making his strange music.

The rain had stopped. The storm drifted above but the clouds had spun aside leaving a hole almost directly above. Lament had cleaned up and had fresh clothes on, his suspenders tight around his shoulders, his arms crossed against his chest as he held the mouth-harp. It took Hellboy a moment to realize that Lament was actively ignoring Jester.

Hellboy kept his gaze on the dark preacher, getting ready for the next game. He said quietly to Lament, "What are you doing here?"

It took a few seconds for him to finish his song. "Oh, I came to help."

"Go on back to Sarah. Don't you want to be there when she gives birth?"

"She's fine. Had the baby without any fuss and hardly no pain. Fifteen minutes and it was all over and done with. Doc Wayburn did little more than watch the proceedings. Granny McCulver's medicines are powerful."

"And the baby?"

"A beautiful girl."

"Congratulations."

Lament merely smiled, but there was a deeper frustration rising into his features now, something Hellboy hadn't fully picked up on before. He remembered then that Lament had never said he was the father of the child.

There was more to talk about but now didn't seem the time. "Anyway, this is my fight."

That got Lament chuckling. His laughter drifted on the breeze, real and wholesome. Jester flinched at the sound of it. "Son, you're a wonder, you truly are. But you can let it go now. This don't concern you."

"Sure it does."

"But it ain't your place. I appreciate your company more than I can say, and you helped out plenty in the swamp there, saved my life you did, but you can go on and get yourself some viddles and rest now."

Viddles?

"You've got to be kidding. I know what I'm doing. You just leave this to me, all right?"

Hellboy stood in a half-crouch, preparing to bound forward. Maybe if he covered the ground between him and Jester fast enough the guy wouldn't be able to pull that mirror routine. Ten feet separated them. All he needed was to get in one good punch. He thought he could make it this time. And if he couldn't, he'd just take another thrashing and come back and try again.

"Stop," Lament said.

Hellboy thought, Ten feet. I can do it easy. I've knocked down ice dragons, twelve-foot-tall werewolves, giant walking stone men, polar bear gods, bridge trolls, cave djinn. He wasn't about to let one gaunt preacher with a silly trick up his sleeve get the better of him.

"Stop," Lament repeated.

"What?"

"Stop fighting. You can't argue the dead back into the ground."

"What's that mean?"

"Exactly what I say. Quit it now."

Like that was even possible. "I never quit."

"When you're playin' a loser's game, you should."

Raising the mouth-harp back to his lips, Lament played on. Hellboy watched Brother Jester over there, and he did look dead. Hellboy had fought zombie hordes before, and a couple of immortal magicians that just kept resurrecting themselves, but he'd never felt like his enemy might truly be trapped just this side of oblivion.

The dark preacher stepped up and Hellboy cocked his fist back.

But he'd been out of his element from the beginning with these people. Lament waited so Hellboy decided to do the same. His head was still heavy with the murmurs of the shadows. *Threatened and threat. Hopeful and hope.*

"I want to see my grandchild," Jester said.

Gators roared in the scrub, sounding close. Hellboy hoped he didn't break any kind of spell by engaging Jester in conversation, but he had something to say. "You have no family here."

"I want the newborn."

Genuinely curious, Hellboy asked, "Why?"

"Did you ask me why?"

Lament pulled the mouth-harp away and said, "I reckon your hearing's just fine for a dead man. He asked you, what do you want with Sarah's child?"

"I want to pass on my wisdom, to teach what I have learned. To love and be loved. To hold and be held. To have a family. It is my secret heart." Aiming a talon-like finger, Jester pointed at Hellboy. "It is his as well."

"Sure," Hellboy said. "I think it's pretty much everybody's. That's not much of a damn secret. Did you expect me to be ashamed of that?"

Lips twisting, Jester couldn't seem to answer.

"Now you know why you don't argue with the dead," Lament said.

"Gotcha."

Eyes igniting with black furious power once more, Jester shifted his finger and pointed at Lament now. Sparks and flame played among his fingers. They licked out toward Lament but never reached him. "I know your—"

"Ayup, my secret heart. Not much to take pride in, a thing like that," Lament said. "A man's true heart is between his own sinful soul and the forgiveness of the Lord. The rest is just petty hate. It's how you creep into a good person's life."

"You speak like a preacher."

"Mayhap you remember I done my share, once upon a time." He raised his mouth-harp, plucked it a few more times, then placed it in his pocket. "Same as you. Before you lost your way and found greater satisfaction in ruining lives than in saving them. Or mayhap you don't recollect at all."

"I am not a destroyer. I am the destroyed."

"Call yourself whatever you like. I know you for a jealous, bitter, heart-wrenched killer. I seen your cruel nature rise up."

"I only did as I was bid to do by the Lord."

With no wasted movement, Lament's hand flashed out and he caught Jester with a vicious blow across the mouth.

The dark preacher twirled around once and landed on his back in the mud. He was grinning, but it was a false front. His eyes were spooked. He spat blood and black fire rose where his spittle landed.

Lament said, "Time you took responsibility for your own frailty, don't you think? Instead of blaming Heaven for all your failings?"

Hellboy thought, Now why couldn't I do that? Why couldn't I just smack him in the mouth?

Jester drew the back of his fist against his bleeding lip, and the blood shone on his flesh like a slick of oil. "More sinned against I was—"

"You forget I was there. I watched you murder your wife. You even tried to kill me."

"John, that was . . . an accident . . . an—"

"So you do remember."

"I recall . . . some things . . . but—"

"It was the act of a furious man following his own evil heart."

Turning, Jester saw that the ghost of his wife was there again, standing to the right of Lament—*she'd said she would not appear at Jester's side anymore*—facing away and almost oblivious to the proceedings.

Hellboy saw the woman and knew she was a spirit, and figured it was the preacher's dead wife. But how was she going to help?

Lament saw her too and out of respect, perhaps even affection, nodded his head and whispered to her. "You go on now, you deserve your peace. Don't you worry about this little grief we got here, it'll be over soon."

"Save him if you can," she said, and slowly, very slowly, the way a woman full of love for her embittered husband is likely to finally give up on him after decades, that slowly, she faded into the wind.

"I am alone but for the cold, merciful angels," Jester said. "That's why I need my daughter and grandchild."

"Reckon you ain't never been alone, and that's been the trouble. Like with Saul and David, God blessed you too early on."

Hellboy was antsy, surprised there was so much talking going on. He had a need for action, and all this standing around was getting on his nerves.

But something seemed to be getting resolved, even though he wasn't sure what or exactly how. He glanced up the track and spotted a lot of the swamp folk in the scrub and on their porches and peering from their windows, the party lights glazing their figures. They stood and waited in the palmettos and palm fronds.

Not far from him, lingering back in the emerald hell, he spotted the kid with eyes like an insect, the beautiful girl without bones in her legs, the dwarf with the big feet, and the *really* weird conjoined twins. Somehow, knowing they were nearby made him feel better.

Lament stood tall, a young man strong in the night, making an appeal to the mentor who'd once taught him in the humble ways of helping a neighbor. "You recall your foul doings and they don't tug at your conscience at all. That's why your redemption lies so far from hand. You ain't even asked for forgiveness."

"From you?"

"From God. And you don't remember a whit. I was too late to stop you from murdering your wife. But you were moving off from her and going after the baby in the crib. You don't love Sarah. You nearly murdered her when she was an infant."

"No. No, that's not true."

"After you nearly brained me with a hatchet, I crawled through your house. I prayed for your enlightenment. It was all I could do, bleeding near to death on your rug. But you heard me. You let her live." Lament drew out a knotted piece of rope from his back pocket. "This bring back any memories?"

"Yes. No. What is it?"

"You recollect what happened later that day?"

"No. Yes. I was . . . I was hanged."

"You know who done it?"

"You did."

"No, I was a dying child. No, it wasn't me."

"Bliss Nail did it."

"He was rushin' over to save his woman and daughter, but no, it wasn't him. He showed up a little while later, and watched you danglin' for a bit. No, wasn't him who done it."

Jester's eyes widened, staring at the knot. "No."

"You done it yourself. You lashed the rope around the rafter and kicked off into purgatory. I crawled to you, blinded by my own blood. Bliss Nail was there, watching you swing. He held Sarah to his chest. I'm the one who cut you down. I prayed over you. Bleeding to death, I prayed over you."

"No."

"I ministered to you. I wanted to save you."

"No."

"And the healin' was strong in me. God wanted it so. Couldn't heal myself, but you ... for you ... I tended your body but couldn't do nothin' for your soul. Bliss Nail carried me to his car and got me to Doc Wayburn. And when he went back to that house later on . . . you was gone. You came back. You came back, but you learned nothing from your journey through oblivion."

"No," said Jester, a whine working through his awful voice.

"It's not too late. Ask forgiveness."

"No."

"It's my fault. I brought you back. My secret heart is that I'd never done it. That I'd left you to swing and sent you on your way. But we all got our sins. You're mine, Jester."

They all turned then as the Ferris boys walked up to them, bracketing Sarah and the child, their knives hooking the moonlight.

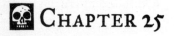

Chapter 25

"Well, here she is," said Deeter, who pressed his stubbled cheek to Sarah's, "the little miss that caused such a stir."

Duffy said, "I been a jot nibbled on, but I ain't complain', preacher. Here's your girl. We done what was asked of us, my brother and me."

Proud of themselves, the Ferris boys leered and drew back, the shotgun aimed loosely in Hellboy's direction.

Lament grinned and Sarah returned the smile. Her movements still held a defiant air, as she lifted the sleeping child and held her closer. Hellboy wondered where it came from, such faith and belief and love in the middle of a hellish day like today. But he already knew the answer. It was the only answer.

"Should you be up and about?" Hellboy asked her.

"When harvest is being brought in, there's women bear their children, then go bring in the sugar cane or tobacco. Or the peanuts. Mrs. Hoopkins wouldn't have let me lay around, I can tell you that for sure."

Brother Jester moved to Sarah as if to embrace her, "Daughter, I'm here."

"Begging your pardon, preacher, but you ain't my father. The man who raised me is in the ground. The man who sowed me is Bliss Nail. I don't see what bloom you've got on me at'all."

"Your mother—"

"The woman who raised me is in the ground. The woman who sowed me is closer to twenty years dead."

Again that unearthly mewl entered Jester's decimated voice. "Your mother was my wife."

"Don't see how that makes me any of yer business, reverend," Sarah said.

"You come two decades and thousands of miles in and out of mountains and valleys for naught, Jester," Lament said.

"But the child—"

"Is mine," Sarah said. "Ain't yours. Nothing here is, though you feel you got a right to whoever and whatever you wanna take. You put your black mark on many. You cursed my half-sisters, the six other daughters of Bliss Nail."

"I did no such thing. His children suffer for his sins, not mine!"

"Who suffers for yours then?"

That seemed to stop Brother Jester for a moment, his eyes puzzled but fierce, as though he'd never stopped to ponder the question before. "I only want my daughter and grandchild."

"She's not your daughter," Hellboy said, gearing up and angling to move on the Ferris boys. He could probably handle a shotgun blast, but he had to protect the girl and the baby. He'd have to be fast.

"Of course she is. She was born from my wife. What else could she be, but my daughter?"

"Her father is Bliss Nail."

"He did nothing but spend a night of lies with a woman not his. His house was too crowded with their voices, that's why he left." As Jester spoke, he rubbed his hands together as if he wanted to clasp his palms in prayer. "And when he returned, their laughter and voices were gone. He called the Word down on himself."

Hellboy said, "I've seen some guys in deep denial, but you, pal, you take the whole freakin' cake."

"I have had wrong done to me!"

"Everyone has. What makes you so special?"

"I am a vessel for the Lord. My enemies called down the whirlwind upon themselves . . . my wife and Bliss Nail. He suffers through his daughters the way I suffer through mine."

"You don't have a daughter," Lament said.

"Mock me no more! I only wish to hold my grandchild!"

The Ferris boys tightened their ring around Sarah, their knives very close to her throat now. As Jester moved, Lament dogged his step, closing the space between them.

"You do this!" Jester screamed. "You blind her to the truth. You're jealous and hoard your child!"

"Me?" Lament said, then added casually, "but I'm not the father."

The grin never left his face but something lurking within him, an inescapable pain, began to bleed out. Hellboy's chin snapped up.

"I was raped," Sarah said, also speaking with an easygoing manner, but the seething anger was barely contained within her. Her long brown hair flowed in the wind, and the silver edging seemed molten beneath the moon. She pointed to the Ferris boys. "By them two right there. Your minions. Your servants. Your lackeys. They done raped me."

Jester's face became wreathed in black sparks. "What?"

Duffy scratched his head. "What's that you say? When'd we do that?"

Deeter said, "I'm havin' trouble recallin' that myself."

Gliding forward, Sarah balled her fist and cracked Duffy in the face. Blood burst and flew from his nostrils.

"Goddamn! You broke my nose, girl!"

"You two morons were drunk on moon. You caught me out at the cemetery, where I was putting flowers on the graves of my parents. You chased me near a mile through the woods."

"We must've had more than a couple'a jugs iffun we didn't take you out to a wooly patch afterward," Deeter said, scratching his chin. "We hardly ever let a gal go."

"Told the sheriff, I did. He dragged them in the next day, hung over, with no memory. They weren't even lyin' when they said they didn't do it, 'cause they couldn't truly recall. And what evidence did I have? A gutter girl with no family, with no man in town, no husband."

"My daughter?" Jester said, trembling, throwing flames. "You two . . . savaged my daughter?"

Sarah stood her ground, shaking her head. "I'm not your daughter."

"Yeah," Deeter said, "She ain't even your kin. Why you makin' such a fuss, preacher? As for savagin', well, we couldn't have done much since we don't remember."

"I suspect it weren't no fun at'all," Duffy mused, "otherwise we'd recollect."

Sorrowfully, Jester said, "You beautiful brothers know nothing of grace."

"Grace Sagamore of the Sag clan?" Deeter asked. "I known her since she was just a little bitty chile."

The acrid stink of burning ozone wafted among them, and heat flashes of ball lightning lit the area. Lament drew Sarah to him, covering the baby. Hellboy had been hit by lightning three times in his life and he really didn't want to go through it again. Jester's hands burned once more and his mouth fell open so that the black fire dropped from his tongue. He smiled at Deeter.

Deeter shrieked, "Reverend, no!" He held onto his Bowie knife unsure of what to do with it, who to threaten, who to stab.

"I am not a preacher!" Jester screamed with his mangled voice. "Defame me no longer!"

Now they were into it.

Knowing what was coming next, Hellboy reached out and tried to get a hand on Jester, but it was already too late. The living lightning inside of Jester framed his body for an instant before it began to leap from him. Duffy screamed and turned tail. Deeter tried to follow but just wasn't as quick. He only got four steps away before the rage erupted from the dark preacher in a brilliant flash of consuming darkness that swept out and blasted the Ferris boy like a thousand frenzied snakes of fire.

The shotgun in Deeter's hand, pointed down, blew his toe off, the same way he'd blown off his father's toe the day he and his brother had murdered the man. It was his final thought before his brain boiled inside his skull and fell out of his ears.

The blazing, biting power snapped at Hellboy and skittered along his flesh. With his right hand he tried to push Lament and Sarah out of the way, but Lament was gone and Sarah and the kid were already huddled in the recess of a nearby shanty doorway.

"You're wrong to hate so much," Hellboy said.

Jester spread his arms wide in a welcoming embrace. "*Brother*."

"I'm not your brother."

"You're my brother in pain and loneliness, in confusion over intent and purpose. You're broken and cleaved."

"Somebody's got to do it."

"You and I are the same."

"Get stuffed!"

"*You cannot hurt me, brother!*"

"I'm not your brother," Hellboy told him. He raised his great stone fist that had shattered mountains and abolished behemoths. And, knowing it would do no good if he tried to crush, smash, slug, or bash the rail-thin dead man with it now, he opened his fist and laid his hand against Jester's chest, and felt the childish angels and human weakness within. "And I don't want to hurt you."

After sprinting a couple hundred yards after Duffy Ferris, with his wounds seeping and broken ribs grating together, Lament dove and tackled him in some laurels. They rolled through a patch of wet scrub oak and came up together knee-deep in mire, facing one another in the night that had brightened with star shine.

Duffy held out a cutting blade and said, "I'm'a gonna skin you like a gator."

"You're gonna take the beatin' of your life, is what you're about to do."

"I reckon I'll bleed you some first, boy."

"You'll bleed, all right."

Duffy Ferris had wrestled gators, killed them, and stripped their heavy skins away. His muscles bulged and he was fast as a striking cottonmouth. He stabbed forward with the knife fully expecting to feel it sliding through flesh.

But there was only empty space. He didn't anticipate Lament being so quick on his feet. Duffy tried again, slashing now and hoping to open up Lament's belly, watch him seep and try to hold his goods in with his hands.

But again, Lament moved too swiftly for him, and Duffy over-extended himself and lost his footing.

He slid in the muck and felt a subtle pressure on his wrist just before hearing a loud snap like a rotted branch breaking. He turned, watched a bright piece of metal fly by, and only hazily noted that it was Mrs. Hoopkins's knife. It landed with a splash in the swamp water while he wondered how the hell he'd dropped it.

Lament stood before him, arms crossed against his chest. Duffy went to throw a fist but an oddly shaped child's arm moved before his eyes. A regular limb bent about halfway in the middle, with the fingers gnarled and wriggling about a bit.

The pain hit a moment later and he realized it was his own arm, busted near in two.

Duffy screamed and howled and thrashed about in the mud. Lament bent to him and said, "We're on gator ground, son, you might want to curb your convulsin' a touch."

Drawing his busted limb as close to his belly as he could, and holding it there tenderly with his other hand, already going into shock, Duffy quietly, almost with a friendly air, said, "Please, don't kill me, John."

Lament said, "Duffy Ferris, I stood over you and your brother on many a night while you snored in your moonshine drunks. I watched you sleep while I slapped an ax-handle in my hand, prepared to cave in your skulls. Many a night it was over the years. The world woulda been a better place, all right. But the Lord let me know it wasn't the right path. I don't aim to understand why He let you go on as long as you did, causin' the evil that you have, murderin' and begettin' your other atrocities, but I held true to my faith even when I wanted to scream. I did my best to see that you had your role to play for the greater good. You hear me, son?"

"I hear ya. But what's all this talk for?" Duffy almost started to grin, but thought better of it. "The Lord God Hisself done already told you to let me be."

"Whatever it was you needed to do, you already done it, 'cause the Almighty . . . well . . . let's just say He ain't so worried about your well-bein' no more."

"But you cain't just kill me!" Duffy cried.

Lament told him, "You deserve it more than anyone I ever met, more so even than Jester. Blessed by God with them fine features and you never done a lick of good in the world."

"Gimme a chance to redeem myself, preacher!"

"I'm not a preacher," Lament said, "and I don't kill. But you got a call to make amends. Like I said, we on gator ground. You've poached these swamps for years, you and your brother and your daddy before you. You've worked for the people that tried to ruin this land. You got a lot to make up for, iffun you're sincere."

"Oh, I am, I am!"

Duffy started to beg again, but as he perched himself in the muck he felt the cutting blade right under his flank. He snaked his hand down and grabbed the handle with his good hand. "I am, I am!" he repeated, and couldn't contain his snicker as he brought he knife up, preparing to jam it into Lament's throat.

Duffy felt a subtle pressure on his wrist just before hearing another loud snap like another rotted branch breaking. He turned and watched Mrs. Hoopkins's knife fly by.

This time the pain hit quicker. Shrieking, Duffy went down and spun under the water, the agony in his two busted arms driving him nearly out of his head. He came up sputtering and coughing and grunting, but couldn't clear the muck from his throat. He began to croak like a gator.

Lament backed away until he was up on grassland, where he squatted and got out his mouth-harp and twanged a tune. Duffy roared and croaked some more.

His own cries called three bulls out from the bog, and one after the other they crawled through the laurels and titi and came down after him. Lament stood his ground and when the gators strayed too close to him, he waved them on toward Duffy, who tried to scramble through the watergrasses and swim away with his two shattered limbs.

Try as he might though, he didn't manage to get very far before the gators set upon him.

They didn't kill him fast. They did what they like to do with their food, dragging it around and pounding it against logs, softening it, taking it down to their mud holes and stuffing it in tussocks of root and bramble, letting it ripen.

When the few straggler bulls came by to raise their heads from the water and stare inland, Lament said, "It's been a rough couple'a days, boys, now don't go makin' it no rougher. You got your supper, so you move on now."

They did, slipping away in one direction while Lament went another.

Hellboy faced Jester, thinking about being the destroyed and the destroyer. He wavered on his feet and saw that Jester was doing the same.

The angels swarmed him, plucking out pieces of him, stinging like wasps. He didn't know if it was going to help. All these years with Jester and they still didn't know anything much about what it meant to stand up and fall down. To love and to hate, to seek out answers in the earthquake and the silence. He was remote and He was not. He was vast and He was not. He was here within both of them and He was. We are. I am. The distance between man and God seemed as wide as ever. Archangels wouldn't be able to close the gap. It was up to man and God to get there on their own. Hellboy figured they'd make it eventually.

Dripping and mud-soaked, Lament appeared at Hellboy's side and tugged at his elbow. Hellboy tried to refocus.

"You all right, son?"

"What?"

"Them shadows been wearin' upon you."

"They have their work to do, same as the rest of us, I guess."

"You got some more fire, son?"

"I've always got fire." Hellboy got out the Zippo and snapped it off his hip again. In the glow, Hellboy saw that Lament held a throbbing black piece of . . . something.

"What do you have there?" Jester asked, roused from his own thoughts. "What is that?"

"This here?" Lament said. "Recognize it? This is a piece of shadow taken from a dead man. He chopped it off himself." Lament held the coursing piece of darkness in his hand. "Murdered his wife with a hatchet. Then threw it down and cut off part of his own shadow."

"My . . . ?"

"Makes me wonder . . . if I give it back, what's gonna happen?"

Jester knew it contained too much of the man he'd once been—the weak and faltering man, the one driven mad, the one denied by Heaven. He backed away a step and moaned because he felt something he had not felt in twenty years. The honest, true, and pure grip of fear.

"You know what I been doing with this portion of shadow right here?" Lament asked. "I been talkin' to it since I was a child. I been tryin' to teach it to follow God's path." He held the piece of darkness out to Hellboy and said, "I can't put it back to him. You gonna have to do it."

"Why?"

"You're stronger than me, and you got more understanding."

The shadow, like a frail animal, made a scrabbling effort to leap from Lament's hand into Hellboy's and failed. It tried again and landed upon him.

I am many things, the man said—the man Brother Jester had been before he'd broken faith. *Weak and willful. In need of great love and consumed by fear that the Almighty has turned His back. The power to sing and heal proves me only a vessel, and my faith is in decline. My wife is too often alone. I miss her dearly. I am a man. I merit my own life, one free from God's constant demands. The distance between us grows greater. I love. I need love. I am a son but I wish to be a father. I want a child. My wife and I deserve a child. God forgive me, I stray from His path and seek my own.* The man wailed because it was what lonely, distressed men do. The man was lost, in need of a family.

Hellboy leaned forward and spoke to the lost soul with as much conviction as he could muster.

He whispered, "Do your best to go and sin no more." Then drove the shadow against the man's chest as if nailing it to him.

Leaning forward as if listening to a soft voice, Jester cast his own shadow beneath the moon and said, "I'm weak and willful, in need of great love and consumed by fear. God forgive me. Oh God, forgive me what I've done. All that I've done." He let out a keening sob.

The archangels rose and moved from him, from within and without him, their feathered wings unfurled and ready for flight.

Lament put out his hand and closed his eyes, dropped his head back and spoke. He said, "I hear you, children. Your ambition's been honest, and for that we thank you. But the gates of Eden need to stay closed for a little while longer. We'll find our way back to God and Him to us. You done your duty. You get on now."

Black wings, they flew into the night toward the rim of the heavens.

Brother Jester, slave to God's noblest efforts, who had returned to the town of Enigma but found his destiny in a nameless swamp village, who had lived and died, now lived again as an ailing, lonely man. He was thankful for the chance. On his knees, he rocked back and forth and hid his face in shame. "Lord, the things I done, the things I done—"

Lament had nearly passed out on his feet, and Hellboy helped him to stand. "You need to rest."

"These damn ribs."

Sarah and her child moved out of the shanty doorway to join them, and the swamp folk stepped from their homes and watched the proceedings, close by but afraid there was still a reckoning due among these powerful few.

Fishboy Lenny swam up and circled Deeter's corpse.

"Okay," Hellboy said, "so what do we do with Jester now?"

Lament said, "Ground's soaked in miracles. Swamp's full of flung-aside crutches. The lame walked here. The deaf heard the word. The blind saw a vision of God. That has meaning. Worth."

"Despite all the trouble he's caused?" Hellboy asked. He wasn't being dissident, he was simply stating a point. "He murdered his own wife. He almost killed you when you were a kid."

"Not in spite of, just sayin' it's the case. He has his role to play for the greater good."

"How do you know?"

Eyes wide, Lament seemed surprised Hellboy would ask such a question. "Because we all do."

"Oh. So what should be done with him now?"

"I don't reckon I know for sure. What's your feelings?"

A dark preacher, once a good man and then a half-demon, burdened with a knowledge he shouldn't have had, fighting himself and trying to forgive himself, and always failing before the faces of angels. Hellboy—who knew a little about what it was like to be burdened with a dual life—didn't know how this situation should play out.

"Let him find his way back to salvation," Sarah said, pressing her face to the bundle in her arms.

Most of the time when Hellboy was done fighting something, that something lay in a pile of rubble or oozing in the sunlight. He wasn't sure what to do with an enemy who was still walking around at the end.

"Okay, so we let him go."

Lament asked, "You sure about that, son?"

"No. But he's not a dead man anymore. Now he's as full of confusion and regret as anybody. It won't be hard to beat him again, if we have to."

"I s'pect you're right about that."

Hellboy walked over and bent down to Brother Jester, and helped the feeble, starved old man to his feet. He said, "Just remember what I said about sinning, or I'll come back and do more than just knock your hat off next time."

"Thank you," Jester said. He kissed Hellboy's right hand, turned, walked into the merciful gloom of the emerald hell, and was gone except for one last quivering word.

"*Brother.*"

 # CHAPTER 26

Hellboy came to the crossroads.

It was mid-afternoon, but the day had been a little rainy, and now as it warmed the mist drifted in off the deep acreage of sugarcane.

He and Lament had spent almost a week in the swamp village, recuperating, enjoying each other's company, and building houses that wouldn't get pushed over in a strong wind.

He'd first played baseball in 1947, but he pretended he didn't know the rules so that the village kids could show him how it was done. They found a flat dry meadow and the pumpkin-headed kid pitched, the insectoid kid was umpire, and Fishboy Lenny played shortstop. Lenny could really smother the ball.

Ma'am McCulver prepared huge meals, and the night before they left they had another genuine hootenanny that wasn't fouled by any uninvited guests or troubles.

Leaving Hortense and Becky Sue behind in the village, where the girls wanted to stay for a while longer with their newborns, Hellboy, Lament, and Sarah said their goodbyes to the swamp folk at dawn and decided, without saying so aloud, to leave together.

They walked to the creek where the Ferris boys' stolen skiff had been beached on the shore and climbed in.

Hellboy was getting used to stobbing and rowing, and followed Sarah's easy directions through the blackwater. Every so often the sound of a loon or an egret would draw his attention to the slough.

On occasion the baby would cough or cry, a vast and lovely sound that filled the stillness.

They picnicked on a bramble island and ate a fine meal of griddle cakes and bacon that Lament cooked. Afterward, Lament played his mouth-harp and Sarah sang along, and with the morning moving away rapidly they were soon back in Enigma.

They were mostly quiet as they hiked the backroads of town, the hush broken only occasionally by a pickup rumbling by. No one offered to give them a ride, and Hellboy didn't think they'd take one anyway. He'd been worried about Sarah being on her feet for so long, but she seemed to enjoy the exercise as the day grew hotter.

"You come up with a name for the little one yet?" Hellboy asked.

"We're thinking of Lila," Sarah said. "After my mother."

He thought on it for a moment, wagged a finger under the infant's chin, and said, "I like it."

Without acknowledgment, but with a deeper understanding of what had to happen next, they walked until the Nail mansion came into view.

This time, the moment Hellboy stepped onto Nail land, he noticed a lifting of the atmosphere. He glanced up at the row of large windows above and saw that none of the six lovely pale women were staring down at him.

Lament turned to Hellboy and told him, "Bliss Nail's her daddy, and she deserves a family, now that the folks who raised her are gone. A family besides me and the baby, a'course. She's got six sisters to gab with now. And ole Bliss Nail gonna have to cough up some of his coffers and quit livin' in the blood of the past. Someone's gotta help pay the bills at Mrs. Hoopkins's peanut farm and take care of the girls."

Hellboy nodded at that and stayed back a bit on the front walkway while Sarah and Lament continued up to the door. Lament spun and said, "What's this?"

"I've got to go."

"You ain't comin' in?"

"It's not my place, John."

"You're wrong about that. You're a friend, and a friend is always welcome."

"Thanks, but you're all a family now, and need time to work things out yourselves."

Sarah moved to him, hugged him, and said, "It's only thanks to you we ever come away from that place intact. We owe you our hearts."

"You don't owe me anything."

"I reckon we'll run into one another somewhere down the line, son."

Lament held his hand out and Hellboy shook it. "Mayhap we will," Hellboy said, and that got both of them grinning.

He watched them step inside, the man, woman, and child, and after a moment heard a swelling of voices and laughter. He didn't even want to bother Bliss Nail and ask for the bus ticket to New York.

As he listened to them, the family meeting in celebration, Waldridge the houseman silently appeared at his elbow.

"Shouldn't you be in there tending to things?" Hellboy asked. Still in his cap and white gloves, Waldridge said, "I'm dead this time. Don't be concerned with me none though, I'll be leaving this earth presently. I just wanted to hear the ladies speak for a while first, and see the new miss come home."

"Well," Hellboy said, "thanks for telling me."

"I knowed you was worried about it."

"Did you at least go peacefully?"

"Happened on the way back from droppin' you off at Mrs. Hoopkins's peanut farm. Heart just stopped workin' at the wheel."

"Did you crack up the Packard?"

"Bite off your tongue, son," Waldridge said. "I eased that car to a slow, full stop with my very last breath."

Hellboy stepped up to the house and peered through a window. The six silent daughters were no longer silent. They were chatty and giddy and fanciful, and Bliss Nail actually had tears in his shining eyes. They all took turns reaching for Lila and making faces. It wouldn't be long before the other six had husbands and families of their own.

The lace curtains flapped and one of the sisters, perhaps the one who'd waved to him before and touched his cheek, smiled at him. Hellboy nodded, then turned away, alone again, and walked back down the road. Soon a pickup heading north stopped on the side of the road and he climbed in back. The rain started to come down again but he didn't mind as he sat there alone with his thoughts, humming quietly to himself.

TOM PICCIRILLI lives in Colorado where, besides writing, he spends an inordinate amount of time watching trash cult films and reading Gold Medal classic noir and hardboiled novels. He's a fan of Asian cinema, especially horror movies, pinky violence, and samurai flicks. He also likes walking his dogs around the neighborhood. Are you starting to get the hint that he doesn't have a particularly active social life? Well to heck with you, buddy, yours isn't much better. Give him any static and he'll smack you in the mush, dig? Tom also enjoys making new friends. He's the author of twenty novels including *The Midnight Road, The Cold Spot, Headstone City*, and *A Choir of Ill Children*. He's a four-time winner of the Bram Stoker Award and has been nominated for the World Fantasy Award, the International Thriller Writers Award, and Le Grand Prix de L'lmaginaire. To learn more, check out his official website: www.tompiccirilli.com.

HELLBOY™

by MIKE MIGNOLA

SEED OF DESTRUCTION
with John Byrne
ISBN: 978-1-59307-094-6 | $17.95

WAKE THE DEVIL
ISBN: 978-1-59307-095-3 | $17.95

THE CHAINED COFFIN AND OTHERS
ISBN: 978-1-59307-091-5 | $17.95

THE RIGHT HAND OF DOOM
ISBN: 978-1-59307-093-9 | $17.95

CONQUEROR WORM
ISBN: 978-1-59307-092-2 | $17.95

STRANGE PLACES
ISBN: 978-1-59307-475-3 | $17.95

THE TROLL WITCH AND OTHERS
with Richard Corben and P. Craig Russell
ISBN: 978-1-59307-860-7 | $17.95

DARKNESS CALLS
with Duncan Fegredo
ISBN: 978-1-59307-896-6 | $19.95

B.P.R.D.: HOLLOW EARTH & OTHER STORIES
by Mignola, Chris Golden, Ryan Sook, and others
ISBN: 978-1-56971-862-9 | $17.95

B.P.R.D.: THE SOUL OF VENICE & OTHER STORIES
by Mignola, Mike Oeming, Guy Davis, Scott Kolins, Geoff Johns, and others
ISBN: 978-1-59307-132-5 | $17.95

B.P.R.D.: PLAGUE OF FROGS
by Mignola and Guy Davis
ISBN: 978-1-59307-288-9 | $17.95

B.P.R.D.: THE DEAD
by Mignola, John Arcudi, and Guy Davis
ISBN: 978-1-59307-380-0 | $17.95

B.P.R.D.: THE BLACK FLAME
by Mignola, Arcudi, and Davis
ISBN: 978-1-59307-550-7 | $17.95

B.P.R.D.: THE UNIVERSAL MACHINE
by Mignola, Arcudi, and Davis
ISBN: 978-1-59307-710-5 | $17.95

B.P.R.D.: GARDEN OF SOULS
by Mignola, Arcudi, and Davis
ISBN: 978-1-59307-882-9 | $17.95

B.P.R.D.: KILLING GROUND
by Mignola, Arcudi, and Davis
ISBN: 978-1-59307-956-7 | $17.95

To find a comics shop in your area, call 1-888-266-4226. For more information or to order direct: •On the web: darkhorse.com •Email: mailorder@darkhorse.com •Phone: 1-800-862-0052 Mon.–Fri. 9 AM to 5 PM Pacific Time.